CITATIONS

CITATIONS

A BRIEF ANTHOLOGY

Edited by
Jasper Siegel Seneschal

USHGURIUD

LONDON | TORONTO

© 2012 USHGURIUD EDITIONS

Published through EVCco Communications
a division of The EVC Company
London, Toronto
ushguriud.evcco.com

Cover design: E. Victor C.

Printed in the United States by Lulu Enterprises, 2013
stores.lulu.com/ushguriud

ISBN: 978-0-9921495-0-5

First edition.

10 9 8 7 6 5 4 3 2 1

"Slave, agree with me!"
"Yes, my lord, yes!"
~ Anonymous, c. 1000 BC
'The Dialogue of Pessimism'

Dedicated.

CONTENTS

CONTENTS

INTRODUCTION

It is a well known fact that, as a civilization grows old, its basic values are in danger of losing their hold upon the individuals who participate in it. Scepticism, doubt, and indifference begin to undermine the spiritual structure which comprises the civilization. Such scepticism toward all values, utter negation of the possibility of a 'good life', begins to make its appearance in Mesopotamian civilization in the first millennium B.C. This scepticism has found expression in a long dialogue between a master and his slave; it is known as the 'Dialogue of Pessimism'.[1]

~ Thorkild Jacobsen, 1946
'Before Philosophy'

An aristocrat languishes in idle boredom. Summoning a slave, he declares his intent to engage in one activity after another so that he might meaningfully occupy his time. The slave praises each suggested task, giving this good reason and that to support his master's plans. But no sooner is each justification made than the master loses interest. His servant, quick to please, then offers counter-arguments against each rejected act so as to bolster his master's fickle whims. Hunting, feasting, coitus, oblation, philanthropy, and political revolution are all considered then dismissed, with each shown to be useful and pointless in equal measure. With every activity now lacking any meaning the master, at last, proposes a murder-suicide with his slave. But futility is discovered even in this, and he is left transfixed in his tedium, no better off than when he began.

So runs the plot of the *Dialogue of Pessimism*, a text which remains one of the more intriguing artifacts of ancient thought. Debate still continues among scholars as to whether the tone of the *Dialogue* was intended to be serious, satirical, or possibly something in between. What cannot be disputed, however, is Professor Jacobsen's assertion that societies, as they age, will inevitably face profound crises of faith in themselves. *Pace*, then, historian William Schermerhorn who, in his 1958 book *Accounts of Progress*, maintained that:

> *Any sufficiently durable culture must risk*
> *falling victim to its own success. Enamoured by*
> *the gains of its longevity, a culture may easily stagnate*
> *in self-satisfaction, eventually to wither for lack*
> *of healthy scepticism, encrusted in a hermetic shell of*
> *unquestioned traditions and dogma.*[2]

Or, perhaps not?

A youth inveighs the common schoolboy refrain of - "*Well, I never asked to be born!*" - and his words are dismissed out of hand as merely a clichéd tantrum of immaturity. Another, however, employs the words of Milton by quoting:

> *Did I request thee, Maker, from my clay*
> *To mould me man? Did I solicit thee*
> *From darkness to promote me?*

and now his parents at least pause to consider the relative profundity of this notion. Knowing his makers to be of a certain literate, if not pretentious disposition, the youth then adds how Shelley just happened to use this same passage as the epigraph to her *Frankenstein*, and so multiplies the credence of his complaint. And yet, even if his parents were oblivious to the works, or even the names of Milton and Shelley, they may still be won over by the tacitly knowing weight implied in this act of borrowing. Such is the power of citation.

Of course, such is also the problem. Whether artistic, aphoristic, or academic in nature, many tend to accept a cited word with deferential ease. The preeminent airs lent by an "*As So-and-so once said...*" will often pass a remark through a page, or conversation, without much inquest. Thus, when posed with conflicting quotations, like those of Messrs. Jacobsen and Schermerhorn, we might seem to be left in the rather ambivalent position of our "master." How is one to assess the role of scepticism in cultural (and, by some extention, individual) demise based solely on the testimony of these two equally reasonable, equally authoritative, and equally unsubstantiated quotes? Are we to go so far as to actually think the matter over for ourselves?

Certainly conclusions may be drawn without too much thought. Either excerpt here could appeal to various pre-existing biases (whether one is of a more conservative or liberal bent, for instance). One could even look to factors entirely outside the content of the quotes themselves - style of writing, regard for the authors' respective institutions, etc. - in order to form an opinion. A less superficial investigation might draw distinctions between the one's use of "culture" and the other's "civilization"; might inquire into either's definition of the term "scepticism"; or might even take into account the historical context of the quotes themselves, noting how the former was written in the wake of the Second World War, while the latter was penned at the height of the booming decade which followed. Beyond that, the reader may possibly hope to ascertain the editor's own preference (should he have one), perhaps seeking clues in the epigraphic location of the former quote versus the interjectional placing of the latter...or what have you.

In the absence of any resolution by these methods, however, and lacking any further wisdom in the matter, one might, at last, look to find some compromise. They might even grow somewhat suspicious of this very diametric. Indeed, the two views may not be mutually exclusive. Both doubt and undue assuredness could well upset the ballance of a functioning lifestyle. Surely then, both Jacobsen and Schermerhorn make valid observations. But what if now I were to tell you that one of these two author's isn't even real? The name, the book, and the quote - all fictions. Would that make the observation any less valid? The question, any less real?

A man is fond of echoing a certain line from Hermann Hesse, until one day he is informed that it was not Hermann, but rather Rudolph Hess who actually spoke these words. Both the line and the sentiment are now discarded. An Englishwoman quotes freely from Nietszche until she goes on to read what he had to say of both the English, and of women. Again, the lines are abandoned. Yet, we do not expect either to abandon the practice of citation itself. Each will soon find appropriate replacements in other sources to confirm, or ignite their predilections. Such is our apparent need for other people's words. But still, they are only words. What is it, then, that is so appealing about taking another's word for it?

Certainly, you would think, there is something of Pope's *"what oft was thought, but ne'er so well express'd"* in it. Or, to quote again from one of history's most quoted books of quotations:

> *Try not with words the talker to outdo;*
> *On all is speech bestowed: good sense on few.*[3]

The above is taken from the first book of Cato's "distichs." For those unfamiliar, Cato was a Roman aphorist of still disputed identity, while a distich is simply a verse of two lines. In other words, a couplet or epigram - which, of course, is not to be confused with the epi*graph*s already encountered here in the form of quotations preceding a text. As somewhat of an even further aside, I should note that Northrop Frye, in opening his essay *Approaching the Lyric*, stated that "*there was a purist in the Greek Anthology who maintained that an epigram is a poem two lines long, and that if you venture on a third line you're already into epic.*"[4] Likewise, one could conceivably argue that when dealing with epigraphs one should limit oneself to no more than a pair, and that if you venture on a third you're already into anthology. Speaking of which, apologies to anyone hoping to read more about the *Dialogue* or cultural scepticism from here on out, but, as an anthology which has already made such liberal use of other people's words before even getting to the anthologized works themselves, I believe we are now closing in on an area rather more central to the premise of this book.

Of course, here might be an opportune place to venture off into the history of anthology itself - into Meleager's floral "*Garland*", or even Polemon's prior collection of epigrammatic epigraphs (or epigraphic epigrams?) - but surely I've ventured too far already. I will only briefly make mention of these two terms' shared etymology - both from the Greek *epigraphein*, "to write on" or "above," in reference to architectural inscriptions (such as those compiled by Polemon) - for, perhaps, herein lies a deeper cause for our concern with other's words. The written language itself has its roots in citation, developed by the hands of scribes rendering content which was rarely their own. The first public inscriptions were quotations of law and decree, passed down from priests and kings, or even the gods themselves. To have ones words recorded at all was, for generations, an absolute guarantee of authority - indelibly carved, as they were, in the imposing stone of some great temple or monument.

Clearly, however, this is no longer the case. Only in more recent times could we declare that something was not worth the paper it's written on. Nevertheless, a hint of vaguely fearful respect may still linger somewhere in our genetic memories to be applied to any words we might happen to face. How else to explain the extreme lengths so many have gone to under the influence of language? History is, of course, replete with examples of writers and orators who have moved both men and nations to kill by the power of words alone. Less common, but perhaps even more striking, are those who have caused their audience to turn this power against themselves. The ancient poets Archilochus and Hipponax are two such raconteurs who were said to have wielded words with such force that they drove their enemies to suicide by the sheer brutality of their invective. On the other hand, there are some who have not shamed, but inspired their public into self-annihilation. According to Callimachus, Plato's *Phaedo* encouraged one Cleombrotus to leap to his death in the Adriatic - yet not before he purportedly convinced hundreds more to do the same through his own rhetoric. A century or so later, Hegesias' philosophical treatise *Death By Starvation* was apparently so well received (and followed) that he was banished from Alexandria by Ptolemy II. Closer to our own time, the infamous plague of "*Wertherfieber*" which swept Europe in the wake of Goethe's *Sorrows of Young Werther* supposedly claimed upwards of 2,000 hopeless romantics. Even more recently *Gloomy Sunday*, a song penned by the Hungarian duo of László Jávor and Rezső Seress, was said to have influenced a few hundred more suicides during the 1930s.

Beyond the powers of authority and persuation, however, perhaps the most appealing aspect of another's words is simply their convenience. Whether distilled in the briefest apophthegm, or spread out across some voluminous tome, the thought is ready-made, the heavy lifting done. It's there to be used like a weapon or tool, and as time wanders on, seemingly leaving us fewer and fewer new things to say, it becomes ever more useful. As technology moves forward, as well, it also becomes much easier. Indeed, in this "information age," where so much is available to so many so quickly that enlightenment nearly verges on light pollution, it can sometimes appear that expression has been reduced to nothing more than a mad race to unearth and claim references. As such, the citation is also there to be donned, like some article of fashion from which we may reap the praise of discriminating taste without ever exerting ourself in the actual toil of manufacture. Of course, if one is feeling particularly creative, one might coordinate a passage or phrase with a few select others to complete an ensemble that may faintly suggest something almost barely original. The entire genre of scholarly writing rests mainly on this principle, where texts consist merely of some brief proposition followed by a cobbled litany of he-said's and she-said's. This patchwork mode of address, worthy of Dr. Frankenstein himself, perhaps found its greatest expression, though, in a classical form of poetry known as the "cento." In this method every single line is an excerpt from another writer's work, removed and rearranged from its proper context so as to convey the centologist's own personal whim. From here, I suppose, one might view the anthology as a sort of novelized cento, with each constituent piece being merely an extended citation. After all, what is the point of assembling such a thing if not to express something through the act of its assembly?

Having come to this point you may assume it is the role of an introduction like this one to explain what the editor is attempting to express through *this* particular anthology. At very least, you would probably expect him, by now, to have touched on the actual works contained in this book; to have outlined what they themselves might be trying to express, and to illustrate what their perceived relation to each other is. All very reasonable assumptions to make assuming the editor, himself, was aware of such things. But if all these rather unfocused musings haven't already made it apparent, the fact is I'm not entirely sure what this anthology is supposed to be about. I had hoped somewhere in the writing of this preface that I might finally glean this little detail; reveal what the works themselves have to say, and why I've brought them all together. But no such luck, so far. At present, I can only tell you that I've done this thing, and was compelled, somehow, to do so.

Of course, there are some ostensible similarities between each of the parts in terms of certain subjects and themes which should become obvious upon reading (this selection was not totally arbitrary, whatever else it may be). But, at a deeper level, it is the underlying message or implication, of each and in sum, which still remains somewhat elusive - if not, perhaps, illusory. After all, there could be no real point to any of it. Indeed, it may well be folly to expect some unified (let alone meaningful) statement from such disparate, random findings - an interview, a school report, a five minute play, an application form, and then all these quotations, citations, and so forth. That these should even share the designation of literature, let alone the pages of any compendium, is questionable at best. I claim no expertise in the writers involved (obscure as most of them are, the reader may well have more information about them than me). I don't even claim to have much affinity for the pieces themselves. They were certainly not all chosen on technical merit. I submit only that this small collection of various words, sutured together and "promoted from darkness," seems to express something which I, myself, can't quite seem to express...for whatever that's worth.

I'll just end by citing a reference to yet another quote. In closing the introduction to the anthology in which the abovementioned Frye essay appears, its editors note how *"Derrida remarked that introductions are always preposterous, written after what they purport to come before."*[5] This introduction may now seem especially preposterous, given the arguably preposterous nature of all that which follows: a brief anthology of obscure works by unknown authors, which may, or may not express something, in whole or individually, about a topic the anthologist has yet to conceive. It should though, if nothing else, serve as some warning to the reader that, after finishing this book, you, like myself - like the master and his slave - may find yourself no better off than when you began. Still, at least, we can say that we've occupied some time. Or, then again, you may choose to keep silent. As for me, I've said my piece.

J.S.S.
Toronto, Sept. 2012

[1] Frankfort, H. et al., *Before Philosophy - The Intellectual Adventure of Ancient Man*, (Chicago, 1946).

[2] Schermerhorn, William, *Accounts of Progress - A Fake Book*, (Unreal, Nonexistent).

[3] Chase, W.J., *The Distichs of Cato - A Famous Medieval Textbook*, (Madison, WI, 1922).

[4] Hosek, C. & Parker P., *Lyric Poetry - Beyond New Criticism*, (Toronto, 1985).

[5] Ibid.

*After the first draught of this poison [...] you probably
imagine that you are going in the direction of the infinite,
whereas you are simply drifting into the incoherent.*
~ Chemist & Druggist, 1868
'On Absinthe'

*After the first glass, you see things as you wish they were.
After the second, you see things as they are not.
Finally, you see things as they really are,
and that is the most horrible thing in the world.*
~ Ada Leverson attrib. Oscar Wilde, 1930
'Letters to the Sphinx from Oscar Wilde'

*I will make a libation to my god.
[...] Now then, what is good?*
~ Anonymous, c. 1000 BC
'The Dialogue of Pessimism'

CITATIONS

FIRST INTERVIEW
Mort W. Lumsden

Readers of *Informem's* debut issue will recall a promise that, in addition to this journal's assemblage of verse, short prose, criticism, and sundry related articles, would be included:

"interviews with the most important and influential literary figures of the day."

In hindsight this may have been a slightly over-reaching promise to make for a small, self-published, regional literature review which has thus far been comprised mainly of submissions from friends of the editor - and read mostly by the same.

To be quite truthful, four issues in, I - *Informem's* aforementioned editor, publisher, art director, contributing writer, and sole financier - am finding the whole enterprise to be a bit more ambitious than I had initially envisioned. Mounting costs and dwindling time to spend has, I'm afraid, put this project's future into some doubt. Indeed, as I write this very piece, there is some doubt as to whether even the current issue will reach press. That being said, I'd still like to consider myself as one who keeps his promises, and, as a man of my word, I should think that one promise of primary importance to keep would be that *Informem Quarterly*, at very least, lives up to its billing as a "quarterly" publication. Therefor, assuming someone other than myself is now reading this, I have somehow - and at some yet untold personal expense - managed to complete this first full volume.

You're welcome, I'm sure.

Looking forward, however, it has become quite

apparent that, should I hope to manage any further volumes, I will have to start turning a profit on this venture. This brings me to that other promise: the interviews. For what better way to attract readership (and thus revenues) than with the lure of a luminary or two, dispensing freely of their wit, wisdom, or (lacking these qualities) their sheer *luminosity*? The problem, of course, is in attracting such people to the pages of this modest little feat. Nine months of relying solely on reputation to bring the luminaries to us has so far proved an insufficient strategy. I have, therefor, since decided to take up the initiative and actively seek some participants out.

Early efforts, I must confess, were somewhat less than fruitful. Beginning right at the top, I quickly found myself back at the bottom following a prompt succession of refusals and brush-offs from various publishers, agents, and even one writer who I managed to get a hold of directly (that is to say ambush at a recent signing). It then occurred that what this quarterly might be lacking - apart from any standing, prestige, or meaningful circulation - was precedent. To interview the "somebodies" one, ideally, should at least have already interviewed, well...*somebody*. So, in the spirit of starting somewhere, *Informem* begins what we hope to be a lengthy series of in-depth and insightful literary discussions in, of all places, a dive bar.

***

To be sure, the Wharncliffe Tavern is not exactly the type of place one would expect to find in-depth, insightful discussions of any kind. Generally speaking, an establishment of this sort, located at the back end of a suburban strip plaza, is not the type of place where one might even expect a decent drink. And, in my defence, I wasn't actually expecting either. Waiting for an overdue batch of *Informem* calling cards to finish printing next door, I was there, initially, to simply kill time. Such is the nature of bars, however, that, aside from being the setting of any number of bad jokes, they are also the perfect setting for a chance encounter. Blood-alcohol levels are elevated, inhibitions are lowered, and people agree to be interviewed by complete strangers. That, at least, is what I assumed happened in our case. In truth, the last clear memory I have of that night was sometime well before our meeting.

From what I recall, I was up by the stools, mulling over the contents of the back bar, plotting my next drink. Hidden away at the rear, abaft some uninspired flight of your standard watering hole fare, I fixed on a curious, rather out of place looking bottle of some unknown spirit. Black and bedusted, label faded and half peeled away, it looked as if it had sat there since before the bar itself was built. "Not unlike him," I might have thought to myself, if my vague recollections are in any way reliable. Cut to some untold period of time later, and the two of us are engaged in a lively discussion of books and writers; miscellanea and etcetera. Just how or why we became so engaged I couldn't tell you now, suffice it to say that through this conversation it was determined that *Informem* had, at last, found it's "somebody."

Now admittedly, as somebodies go, Gerry Vanderson is not likely a name you will immediately recognize. To be perfectly honest, the name is not likely one you would *eventually* recognize either. Indeed, unless you are an avid reader of corporate progress reports, government proposal applications, and other such bureaucratic ephemera, you will probably not be familiar with the name at all - and even then... However, before one starts getting the idea that *Informem's* first published interview consists only of some drunken, bar-room prattle with a randomly met businessman, having no literary relevance whatsoever, let me assure you that this is only partly true.

Gerry is, indeed, a man of business. But it's just that business which provided the impetus for our interview. As proprietor of *F.L. Vanderson Translating Services Ltd.*, Fitzgerald Leopold "Gerry" Vanderson is an individual with some 30 years of practical experience in a field that, content aside, should be very much relevant to any lover of world literature or language in general.

Personally, as a mere monoglot, I know I've always had a certain grudging admiration for the multi-lingual among us. It's an admiration ever reinforced by those constant reminders that "no English translation can ever do justice to *What-have-you*," or how "one can only truly appreciate *So-and-so* in the original Garhwali." Indeed, due to such perceptions, the topic of translation calls forth a whole host of compelling literary matters - from the basic process of how a translator decides on which words to use, and which way to use them, to deeper issues of linguistic relativity, or whether there are certain words, phrases, and even concepts which simply cannot be translated at all. As you will see, though, translation was not the only subject we managed to touch upon here. Vanderson, extremely well-read in a number of areas, was keen to propel the conversation into some rather unexpected places (and, ever more so as the night, and drinks, went on).

Still, the over-arching theme of our talk remained - at least, from what I took away from it - mostly within the purview of this journal. Actually, one might consider this entire article to be something of an exercise in translation itself - or perhaps, more properly, in decipherment. As it happens, I was able to document our discussion on a quite convenient, but rather low quality portable voice recorder which I had only just begun carrying (in, I suppose, the deluded/desperate hopes of stumbling across an errant Booker recipient, or Nobel laureate, casually strolling the streets of Old South). Add to this the noisy backdrop of a crowded bar, with the mounting effects of its wares on the both of us, and you can imagine the difficulties in transcribing the resultant audio.

Nevertheless, I have attempted to capture, as best I can, all of the words, pace, and tenor of our chat - down to every detectable pause and interruption. Still, I can make no claims to a fully verbatim rendering. This is only a faithful-as-possible decoding, from muddled "*Inebrish*" to a mostly comprehendible "*Soberese*." Frankly, some of the dialogue towards the end became so unintelligible that any interpretation of the meaning or intent presented here should probably be taken with a generous rim of celery salt. My apologies in advance, then, to Mr. Vanderson for any mistranslations on his behalf. If I learned anything from our chat, it is that translation is a tricky matter at best, so if I err in any way I trust he'll understand.

Now then, without any further ado, let us pick up the discussion from where the recorder picks it up, abruptly and ambiguously as it does...

FV: — no, lower than that.

ML: Well... Oh, wait...I think that's it here.

FV: Let me get you refilled while you figure that —

ML: No, I think I've got it running now... *Testing, testing...* It looks to be working, at any rate.

FV: Should we start again?

ML: No, no. I'm sure I'll remember... Actually, just go back to what you were saying about the translations of 'translate'.

FV: About...?

ML: The words, in other languages —

FV: Oh, the Romance words?

ML: Right.

FV: *Traduire, tradurre, traducir* - how they come from the Latin *traduco* —

ML: Right.

FV: The same root from which, of course, we get 'traduce'.

ML: Yes.

FV: And so it follows that all us translators must be liars, to some extent.

ML *[laughing]*: Right, right... So, let's start there then. Are you?

FV: Evil beasts and slow bellies.

ML: Slow bellies?

FV: A biblical term...or Greek, rather.

ML: Biblical?

FV: About the Cretans and —

ML: Oh, that liars paradox, right?

FV: That's it. Epimenides...or St. Paul, anyways. Or, wait, was that Eubulides?

ML: So I shouldn't believe a word you say, then?

FV: Only if I start speaking in other tongues.

ML *[laughing]*: OK. Well, that shouldn't be a problem since I can't understand any others. I think I know what you're saying though. At least, from what I've heard...you always read about the problems of trying to translate something like a pun or a poem... I suppose a bit of "lying" is necessary now and again.

FV: It's never quite the truth in the end.

ML: I can imagine. I think I actually might have heard that thing about "*traduco*" and "traducing" somewhere else before.

FV: Oh, I'm sure. It's a ripe old chestnut within the

trade.

ML: Well, I don't know many translators, or much about translating. I did read that George Steiner book though...what was it? Years ago. Perhaps that's where I picked it up. You must have read it also?

FV: *Babel*...something, sure. That's on my bookshelf somewhere.

ML: And his theory that all communication...all understanding is, in a way, an act of translation. Wasn't that it?

FV: Translation, interpretation, hermeneutics... Gadamer also, I think, in...now what was his book? He was writing about that too, around the same time...maybe a little before Steiner. I suppose you could say both had their own "translations" of the idea.

ML: Indeed!

FV: Literally too, I guess...or did they both write in German?

ML: I think Steiner is French, isn't he?

FV: Oh, that's right. But he wrote in English, the original, didn't he?

ML: Right. Though I'd assume he also did the French edition.

FV: You'd think so.

ML: So what's your take, then, on Steiner's...or Gadamer's assertion? I suppose if translation is all a lie like you said, and if you believe them too, then pretty much everything else is, isn't it?

FV *[laughing]*: I suppose. I don't know. I'd believe either of them before you believe me. It's not all really a lie. Translation, anyway. Just not quite the truth, like I said. It's a compromise...with the truth, so to speak. You do what you can.

ML: Oh, I wasn't being serious. I'm sure every translation will have it's own sort of truth as well...in it's own way, if that makes any sense?

FV: It makes it's own sort of sense.

ML *[laughing]*: Thanks.

FV: No, it's just a very tricky business...or can be. Like you were saying about puns, or any *double entendre*... There, in fact - if you want tricky, take on an inkhorn or two! Have you ever tried rendering any last-century French into English?

ML: Never had the pleasure.

FV: Back then, for a time you see, it was quite fashionable to employ the occasional anglicism as a sign of sophistication...or pretension. Just as today one might find '*le mot juste*', *en français*... Isn't that an odd one, by the way? Using one language to refer to the 'right word' in another? I always found that strange... But anyways, you can imagine the kinds of problems this raises for a translator.

ML: How so?

FV: Well, to begin with, shouldn't you wonder why anyone would bother to translate something which has already been translated for you?

ML: I should, I suppose.

FV: But, of course, if you wish to preserve any of the cultural, historical, or stylistic connotations expressed through the use of a foreign phrase you *must* translate, somehow.

ML: True... Would you just reverse the two languages, then?

FV: And translate the words which have already been translated back into the language from which you're translating the rest?

ML: Yes?

FV: You could. But then why would any sophisticated Parisian of the age use any familiar old French expression to properly portray his sophistication?

ML: Right. I guess you could...choose another language altogether, then. Couldn't you?

FV: You could. But which one? And how could any other language possibly address the very specific use of English, reflecting the very specific fashions of that very specific place and time?

ML: So how does one go about translating such a

thing?

FV: Oh, any of the ways you've suggested are generally acceptable; often paired with some unseemly footnote explaining the whole convolution.

ML: That is a tricky bit of business.

FV: Well, thankfully, the average research proposal tends to be a little less involved than all that.

ML: I should hope so! I imagine that type of fare is convoluted enough on its own. But now...well, let's get back to the beginning here. I can't imagine that's the sort of stuff you got into translating for. I mean... well, perhaps I shouldn't assume —

FV: No, that's alright. I didn't...well, I never really intended to get into translation to begin with. I doubt many people do, to be honest. It's just one of those jobs you sort of end up in, I guess. Like accountancy ...or politics.

ML: So how *did* you end up in it?

FV: The same way most do, I suspect. By wanting to become a writer.

ML *[laughing]*: Naturally.

FV: But, of course, those who can't - and can't teach - translate.

ML: Or publish literature reviews.

FV *[laughing]*: That too?

ML: Well, let's not get into my life story... So what exactly led you from one to the other?

FV: Oh...life, responsibilities...the usual things. You know how it is. Over time ambitions become... recreations, and then —

ML: I understand.

FV: Having something half-way interesting to say probably wouldn't have hurt either.

ML: It's never too late, though. Maybe this is your chance now.

FV: What, to say something interesting? About translating?

ML: Why not? I mean, hopefully —

FV: You think I've gained some profound insights from my years of translating conference agendas and...leadership seminar notes?

ML *[laughing]*: Well...

FV: I don't really think I have any deep musings on the matter. None of my own, anyway. Nothing I could tell you that you probably hadn't already read in Steiner, or elsewhere, I sure.

ML: Even still, don't we "often need more to be reminded than informed," as Wilde once said...or someone?

FV: Johnson, I think that was.

ML: Samuel Johnson? Well, one of those fine old aphorists, anyway.

FV: It's been years since I read that book myself, or any such thing. I'm not sure I could discuss the matter very intelligently.

ML: Well, just go back to you, then.

FV: I still can't quite fathom what your interest is...

From here run several more minutes of prodding and appeals for Vanderson to open up on my part, and much reconsidering of whether or not to continue the interview on his. In an attempt to ease the growing tension we paused briefly to replenish our provisions. During this little abeyance Vanderson graciously advised not to let the contents of the bar fool me. "They've got a great stock hidden in back," he said. "Just ask, they'll make you anything."

I asked what he was getting and he mentioned a brand of scotch I was unfamiliar with called Pinwinnie, along with a local brand of chinotto called Brio which I'm quite familiar with from any number of corner pizza places in town. "It's an acquired taste, I'll grant you," he said, to which I politely replied that, for now, I'd stick to my Gilbey's and Canada Dry. Sufficiently rehydrated then, Vanderson at last got on with his introduction to the business...

FV: I was probably in highschool, grade 9 or 10, just

beginning to take an interest in writing. I happened to hear a radio program on the CBC with Northrop Frye. He was talking, among other things, about the way language affects the way we think and express ourselves...something, I think, he termed "automatic fluency," where one's mode of expression becomes so routine or conventional that it manifests as clichés and platitudes...ultimately, bad writing. He then suggested that the best way to combat such an effect - to look at words...and the world itself a little differently - was to learn another language. So, I did. From there I began taking my French classes all the more seriously.

ML: I see.

FV: Perhaps a little too seriously, actually. I barely scraped by in most other things. Languages gradually became the only subjects I could really make any sense of. By my last year of highschool I was taking as many courses as were offered simply to graduate. French, German, Latin...English, of course. From there my fate was pretty much sealed.

ML: As a translator?

FV: As something *wordy*, at any rate. I went into university still fully intending on writing my way back out into the world. Maybe start out in journalism, freelance my way through some far-away lands as I wrote a novel or two on the side... You know, that whole thing.

ML: Of course.

FV: But I was paying my own way through school...

up in Ottawa, where there was no shortage of departments and ministries looking for translators —

ML: Right, right. Then, all of a sudden, here you are.

FV: A likely story, I know.

ML: No, no. I've been there...still am, really. It's all too easy to get caught up in the gears. But it can't be all that bad either. Even in what you do, I mean, there must also be a creative side...an art to it, as it were...isn't there?

FV: An art? No...well, perhaps only in spite of itself. Any "creativity" is simply a last resort. Good translation aims more towards science, or mathematics. Rendering as precisely and faithfully as possible is the goal...or should be. "Licence is for poets, not translators," as one of my old employers was fond of saying.

ML: But some license is surely taken. As you said yourself, it's never quite the truth. Something of your own must be going into it somewhere.

FV: Never purposefully. It's art, you see...or, rather, the self-styled *artist* who'll more often get in the way of good translation. Passing over the obvious word because it's "too obvious"...refusing any help or collaboration so as to express some "singular vision"...needlessly re-butchering a work that's already been done over by a dozen others just for the sake of something new... I guess I'm talking more about literary translators here. I'm, of course, more of an industrial or, what they call these days, a "pragmatic translator." I'm not paid to be clever, so I should probably mind my own affairs here.

ML: No, please - don't mind them on my account! This is exactly the stuff I'm sure my readers would be interested in hearing.

FV: No, really...I'm talking over my head. Sour grapes is all. Believe me, I've tried to get into more literary, or scholarly material myself over the years. But to do that sort of work you generally need to be more of an expert in the writers, or the subject matters being translated, than in the languages themselves. I wouldn't count myself as an expert in anything.

ML: Nothing?

FV: I've never really aimed to be more than an amateur...dilettante...*hobbyist* in any of my pursuits. I'm sure that didn't much help my writing career either. I guess I've always been more of a quantity over quality type. I figure, why put in all the time and effort to become an expert in *one* thing, when you could spend it just as well dicking-around in a hundred others?

ML *[laughing]*: So you're a man of many interests, I take it?

FV: Many interests, few passions...jack of all, master of none. But I'm always trying to learn new things. Making up for school, in a way, I suppose. Of course, most of what I know of the world I've learned through translation...or reading whatever language I was trying to teach myself at the time...

which, when you think about it, somewhat puts into doubt how much I've ever really learned about anything.

ML: Oh, I'm sure you know your trade well enough... Wouldn't you, at least, consider yourself an expert in that, then? In the languages —

FV: Again, quantity over quality. None of my clients will be reading this, right?

ML *[laughing]*: I can't make any promises.

FV: No, I'm fairly competent when it comes to that, I suppose. But then, proficiency in any language is relative. I know just enough I need to in the languages I earn a living from...and just enough that I want to in any others.

ML: And how many others - or, all-told - would that be, exactly?

FV: Well, that's a bit of a difficult question, actually. There's a few I can read, write, and speak fairly well. Then there's a few I can only read, and only somewhat well; and a few more that I used to know but have pretty well forgot. In all, though, I've probably tried on around 20 or so.

ML: Twenty!?

FV: But that sort of depends on how fine your definition of 'language' is, too. You could say I'm fluent in both Metropolitan French and Québécois... though I'm sure there's a few *joual* expressions I'd be unfamiliar with. I also picked up a little Savoyard on a trip to Switzerland once —

ML: These would be more considered dialects, though, wouldn't they?

FV: Well, there's some who'd contend that any languages within the same family - phylum, even - are merely dialects. You could say that French is only some matured strain of Vulgar Latin...by way of the Gallo-Romance, and *langues d'oïl...* themselves all the various *patois* of Italic, Indo-European, Proto-Indo-European, and so on. In that light, French and Italian, English and...Norwegian, are all basically one and the same. To truly expand your vocabulary you'd have to venture out into Ojibwe, or Korean. Sokoro...or Tundra Nenets —

ML: And have you?

FV: Oh, I've tried my hand at some fairly obscure tongues, so to speak. Not much more than dabbling. I've stuck mainly to the "Aryan" families, as we used to call them...though I did take a fairly serious interest in Chinese at one point.

ML: Ah. Cantonese, Mandarin...?

FV: The written language. It's basically the same...at least, before simplification, with all of the dialects... if you can call them that. It was specifically the writing, in fact - the *hanzi* characters - which interested me. Following Frye, I guess, I'd heard, or read somewhere, that they actually shaped Chinese thought in quite different ways from our own...with our phonetic, alphabetic system.

ML: How so?

FV: Something about a difficulty in producing counterfactuals...or "possible worlds," as linguists are wont to say. Their pictographic, ideographic nature - 'person' as a stylized stick figure, for example...or 'death' as a person next to a pile of bones - supposedly this set the Chinese mind to a far more concrete...*pragmatic* way of thinking. But also, as the theory goes, to a more rigid, less creative way of thinking than ours, with our abstract, hypothetical ...interchangeable, rearrangeable relationship with letters, words, and concepts.

ML: I'm not sure that's a trade-off I'd wish to make.

FV: I suppose as a "pragmatic" translator the notion appealed to me at a certain level. All the...arcane vagaries one deals with in my business - in language generally... All those overly complicated, overly specific, yet...persistently ambiguous words... This dependence...*exultation* even, of analogy and metaphor... I don't know. It all seems a little too creative, too imaginative...*imaginary*, sometimes. Do you know what I'm saying?

ML: Not exactly, no.

FV: Well, I'm probably just being overly complicated myself. But then, it was Confucius, after all...or Mencius, or someone like that who said "the enlightened man is always critical of words." I guess I just liked the idea of a firmly rooted language. One that meant what it said, and was clear about it.

ML: And is that how you found it...Chinese, that is?

FV: Not really. The vast majority of *hanzi* are actually phonetic as well...or, at least, involve phonetic elements...radicals. It's all based on system of almost metaphorical sounds. Beyond which there's quite enough syntactic and contextual methods to produce words and worlds just as "possible," or *impossible*, as ours. The whole theory, I think, is more of a "counterfactual" itself.

ML: I see.

FV: But, perhaps, I never quite understood it properly. I may well have only read about it in Chinese, come to think of it. Truthfully, I never really learned enough of the language to draw any solid conclusions. Now it's just another of those I've mostly forgotten. I guess, if you're looking for a firm number - getting back to your original question - I'd say there's...maybe only 4 or 5 languages that I'm really comfortable with.

ML: That's still four more than me! Than most —

FV: But even then, when you're talking about *really* speaking a language...really *thinking* in another tongue, I'm not sure I've ever quite done that myself. I'm not sure I'm ever doing more than just translating ...into English or out of it, on the page or in my head. Perhaps I've only ever been fluent in English... "automatically" so, at least. I certainly was never able to shake those clichés and platitudes...another strike against any authorial pretensions I might have had.

ML: Well, I still think there's a bit more authorial, or artistic merit in what you do than you're letting on.

FV: A pragmatic translator of "*bureaucratica*" would pretty much have to be at the lowest rung on the artistic ladder...if it's on there at all.

ML: But even that carries a certain nobility...a grand tradition. Isn't it said that the written word itself began somewhere in bureaucracy...administration, and accountancy? The very first scribes, record-keepers of the earliest empires!

FV: That is true. Still, I certainly wouldn't consider myself an "artist." An *artisan*, perhaps, as Beckett, I think, once made the distinction...or that might have been Beckett quoting Proust... Regardless though, as I said, art really isn't what the translator should aspire to... But again, I'm probably speaking out of school. The documents I deal with aren't exactly works of art to begin with. Perhaps they simply don't inspire the "artist within."

ML: So you're never tempted, then, to take the odd liberty with some market research...*whatever*?

FV *[laughing]*: And break it up into...dactylic pentameter, or something? They might actually appreciate that, once in a while. You never know.

ML: Well, I was just thinking how every so often you'll hear about some dreadful book, or a movie or something, that'll go unnoticed at home, but then it's translated —

FV: And it becomes a masterpiece?

ML: Right.

FV: I'm not sure how often that actually happens.

ML: No, I can't think of any examples off hand.

FV: Of course, an old saw in one culture can always be a revelation in another...no matter how it's worded.

ML: That's true. I'm sure not many truly dreadful books make it to the translation stage, anyway.

FV: Oh, you'd be surprised. And classics, of course, they'll get churned-up again and again. I think there must be over a hundred English versions, or revisions, of Homer out there...and at least 500 of the Bible. I've heard another update of *À la recherche*, speaking of Proust, is currently in the works as well.

ML: All 3,000 pages, all over again?

FV: There's always something found wanting by someone. No translation is ever perfect - as any translator will be the first to tell you. Why else should every translation you read begin, or end, with some "note on the translation?" But that doesn't seem to stop them all from trying, again and again ...as if enough variations, piled one upon the other, might finally equate, in some way, to a finished, flawless piece without need of explanation.

ML: "Grain upon grain, one by one, and then there's a heap...the impossible heap," just as Beckett wrote himself...didn't he?

FV: Precisely! That was from...*Play*, wasn't it? No...
Endgame. But, of course, he referred there to Zeno's
heap - or was that Eubulides too? - where no number
of grains can ever complete the pile. And perfection,
like a 'heap'...like so many words...it's all just too
vague to be realized, in a way...to be real.

ML: But Beckett, now, didn't he translate his own
works? If anyone could do a flawless translation of
Beckett, I mean... Well, he'd certainly come closer
than anyone else, no?

FV: How close, though? A writer so fond of puns
and word-play as him... He, of course, was always
making changes in his translations, too - adding bits
here, deleting parts there...switching references
around to suite whichever audience he was
translating for...sometimes not bothering to translate
certain parts at all... Hardly flawless.

ML: But artistically, at least —

FV: I'd be interested to know just how satisfied he
ever really was...artistically or otherwise, with any
of his translations. He actually took on an outside
translator eventually...I believe. A South African,
wasn't it? I'm not sure if he did the French to
English, or English to French. Being South African,
however, it could be that neither were even his first
language! Funny that... In any event, I suppose he
must have been satisfied enough to have them
published. As long as the gist comes across, anyway.

ML: Only the gist?

FV: That's all you can hope for at the end of the day. All you *should* hope for, really. This is what I mean about art and everything...you really can't win for losing with it. If you get too clever, wielding license and takings liberties, you'll end up completely divorced from the source material. But then, paradoxically enough, you can end up just the same way by keeping too much to the original; trying to maintain this aspect or that...shoehorning in some parlance or stylistic feature that simply doesn't fit in another tongue. What's lost in translation is mostly the artistry...the subtlety and cleverness...inside jokes and knowing winks to the native reader; all that was never meant to be translated in the first place.

ML: But, surely, I'm getting more than just "gist" when I read Beckett, or...Chekhov, or Kafka, or... whoever.

FV: In English, you mean?

ML: Yes.

FV: Well, some gists are certainly better than others. A good enough story, or idea, should be able to withstand any half-way competent translation. Translation alone, though, can never make a masterpiece...not even add to it. It can ruin one, certainly, if it's bad enough. And, you know, it can also expose one for what it really is...clear away all the jargon and flowery filler; reveal the quality of what's actually being said.

ML: "Un-muddy the waters," as it were?

FV: Indeed. And believe me, it's not just the poets, or Nietzsche, who try to seem deep. All the buzzwords and policy-speak I have to wade through —

ML: You must need a translator yourself at times!

FV *[laughing]*: I should inquire to see if Beckett's is still available. In a way, though, that actually gets easier over time. Eventually they all seem to adopt each other's..."*cubicle cant.*" You know, I'm old enough to have seen the French *l'art logistique* - the lodging of troops in war - introduced to the Anglo workplace as 'logistics', then back into French as... the art of managing office supplies.

ML: Is that right?

FV: Perhaps it's a tad more succinct than the old *gestion des fournitures*...but, I have to admit, I preferred it the old way. I prefer "managing office supplies" for that matter... Well, as much as one can.

ML: It is a bit clearer.

FV: But, of course, 'managing' and 'office' and 'supplies' were all strange new terms at one point, too. You've got to change with the times. No point in...now who was it? Was that Orwell or H.G. Wells who'd have had us all to return to Saxon English? I'm always confusing the two.

ML: I always get Orwell and Orson Welles mixed up myself.

FV: Well, in any case, the language is always evolving. We have no *Académie* to bar the doors against new up-starts, or foreign invaders. Not that it helps the French much, either.

ML: Ah, that's right. They have some official governing body over there to protect the language, don't they?

FV: It has no legal authority, of course...but yes.

ML: So they're not as strict as in Québec?

FV *[laughing]*: Well, that's a bit different.

ML: There's surely nothing wrong with the odd loanword, or portmanteau, every now and then... I mean, that's a French word itself, isn't it?

FV: 'Portmanteau'? Actually...no...well, not in that sense, anyway. That was Lear...or, Lewis Carroll's doing, if I'm not mistaken. From *Jabberwocky*...or about *Jabberwocky*.

ML: It certainly sounds French.

FV: Oh, it was, originally. It's a type of suitcase, or travelling bag... I suppose the metaphor being that of a word to carry different sounds and meanings.

ML: So what would the French word for 'portmanteau' be, if there is one?

FV: That would be...*mot-valise*, in fact. Literally, 'suitcase word'.

ML: So they use an English metaphor, from a different French word, for the same thing?

FV: There's a similar situation with 'malapropism', come to think of it. That comes from a character's name in an old English book or play, I believe...not sure who, or which... But it's based on the French *mal à propos*, or 'inappropriate'...whereas the French term would be *impropriété d'un mot*...or *de langage*. Though, occasionally, you'll see it as *malapropisme*, too.

ML: I suppose that's one way around the old Academy...using their own words against them!

FV: I suppose so. But, of course, if its a war of words we're having, the French have already infiltrated us far more, I think, than we ever will them...largely thanks to the Normans; 1066 and all that.

ML: The sword being mightier than the pen in that instance.

FV: Quite. But the influence has continued long since then. I'm sure you've read things, no more than a few decades old, still spelling 'role' with a *circonflexe* over the 'o'.

ML: Yes, that's right!

FV: And even today, there often remains an *accent aigu* in 'cliché', or —

ML: That little *umlaut* over the 'i' in 'naïve', sometimes...or whatever it is in French.

FV: A *tréma* in that case, or diaeresis.

ML: You'd see that in 'cooperation' too, not long ago.

FV: Right...although that's more of an obsolete English feature. Nothing to do with the French, I don't think.

ML: Gone the way of Saxon?

FV: Like I said, the language is evolving...ever changing. Accents and grammar, pronunciations and spelling... Words come and go, change their meanings...sometimes lose them completely. My own name, in fact, is such a case - an anglicisation of the Dutch *Van Deursen*, a town in the North Brabant region.

ML: Is that right?

FV: It is. Of course, 'Vanderson' is a fine enough name, but —

ML: It's sort of meaningless now.

FV: Right.

ML: It still has a nice ring to it, though.

FV: Well... Now, actually 'nice', come to speak of it, has lost its meaning too...or changed. You know, it originally meant something stupid or silly.

ML: Really?

FV: And 'silly', as a matter of fact, once meant to be merry or blessed... Then 'merry', for that matter, once meant something short-lived —

ML: I know 'humour'...that was, at first, a term for bodily fluids, wasn't it?

FV: It was. Whereas 'tragedy' stems from the rather humourous concept of a singing goat.

ML *[laughing]*: From a what, now?

FV: To 'soothe' once meant to be honest...'awful' once meant something glorious. A 'toilet', like a *portmanteau*, was a bag to carry clothing in - and 'diaper', the patterned fabric from which that clothing might well have been made.

ML: Is that so?

FV: Oh, I could go on! 'Pretty', for instance, once meant to be cunning, or tricky...just as 'glamour' was once related to witchcraft...from the same source as 'grammar', interestingly enough. And it can all seem a bit...*witchy*, this business of words, can't it? Wasn't it Wittgenstein who called the very act of naming an "occult process?" That we "ever seek to bind the inscrutable by the *spell* of a word."

ML: Wait...Spengler, wasn't it?

FV: Was it? Now why did I think it was Wittgenstein?

ML: Oh, you could be right actually. But this gets into another interesting area...with everything always changing, there's quite a bit of translation to do even within the same language, at times, isn't there? Be it Old English to modern, or...office talk, technical jargon, or legalese to regular speech.

FV: Even between people using the same kind of speech there's always a certain amount of translation required. And even then its never quite perfect.

ML: How do you mean?

FV: Well, simply the various connotations that a word can conjure among different people, depending on their own experiences and situations.

ML: Ah, like how...'December' will have a different feel depending on whether you live in the northern or southern hemisphere?

FV: Right. Or how...'marzipan' will have a different *flavour* depending on if you're fond of almonds, or not.

ML: Or if you don't even know what marzipan is.

FV: Exactly! What else...? 'Downtown' will have slightly different...orientational implications to someone living in Byron, and someone coming from Pottersburg...or Masonville, or White Oaks.

ML: Or someone who actually lives downtown.

FV: Precisely... And 'White Oaks' itself, come to mention it, would have a different meaning to one familiar with the De la Roche novels, and one who may see it as only another...generically leafy, suburban brand.

ML: So with all this translation continuously occurring, on all different levels...I guess the big question is if there are things that simply can't be translated - that is, where not even the "gist" can come across?

FV: That is the classic question within the field.

ML: A *cliché*, I'm sure...with, or without the accent.

FV: Well, there's certainly some things which can't be translated very well... For example, certain pidgins and creoles have vocabularies of only a few thousand words...sometimes less. English, on the other hand, may have upwards of a million...no one's really sure. I think there's at least 600,000 in the latest *OED*. So now imagine trying to translate the complete *Oxford English Dictionary* into some... Malay-based creole - as bizarre an undertaking as that might be in the first place. It just wouldn't work out very well. Or, at very least, it would make for a rather redundant read.

ML: I'll bet. And then, what would a French-to-English dictionary look like in Malay?

FV: Quite bizarre as well, I'm sure.

ML: From an English perspective, though - as big a language as it is - what about when you hear how the Germans, or whoever, have a particular word for this or that, of which there's no word in English. Like... *schadenfreude*, or what-have-you?

FV: Another classic cliché!

ML *[laughing]*: Why thank you!

FV: That's... Well, but then, it's all a bit cliché, in a way, now isn't it?

ML: What is?

FV: Well, wouldn't it seem the Germans themselves don't really have a "word" for *schadenfreude* either?

ML: I'm not sure I follow.

FV: They have a word *schaden*, meaning 'to harm' or damage, and *freude*, meaning joy or pleasure. Then they've simply thrown the two together, in the lack of anything new to say.

ML: A compound, right.

FV: Right, a compound. And in German, of course, such constructions are rather obvious. But it's the same process in any language...separate words that acquire, over time, the appearance of one...of something unique. Yet there's nothing uniquely German about the concept of *schadenfreude*. Nothing to stop us from having coined something along the lines of "*harmjoy*," or what-have-you. Then again, there's nothing stopping us from just using the German word instead, which we already do... Take out another loan, as it were...in the lack of anything new to say ourselves. You see? All words, all language...it's all sort of cliché at its foundations.

ML: But not all words are compounds, or foreign borrowings.

FV: They mostly are...from somewhere, or something else. We could go on to break-down the *schaden* and the *freude*, too, if I had my *Kluge Wörterbuch*. I believe, though, *freude* comes from something to do with running, or jumping...a dead metaphor, anyway - another major source of words. But where are the truly new and unique words? It's always some truncated old phrase, some compound or kenning...allusions and analogies, so used and reused that they've wormed their way into the lexicon by the sheer force of their...banality.

ML: I see what you're saying. But, of course, we couldn't have a completely unique and distinct word for everything...every object or occurrence. Our brains...our tongues, just couldn't deal with it.

FV: True. But...one might wonder, do we really have a unique word for anything?

Vanderson here went on to explain the intricate etymologies behind a number of English words, including the 'black pants' he noticed me wearing. Starting with how 'black' was actually a reference to the effect of charring - from the Indo-European root *bhleg*, meaning 'to burn' - he went on to tell of how 'pants' are, of course, a shortening of *pantaloons*, an Italian reference to the type of trousers reportedly worn by a Byzantine saint - one *Pantaleon* - itself a name of Greek origin approaching something in meaning to 'all-compassionate'. So, in conclusion, to claim I was wearing a pair of 'black pants' would, in Vanderson's estimation, be tantamount to claiming that I had donned the charred remains of a benevolent Christian martyr. I didn't quite have the heart to point out that my pants were more of a navy blue.

FV: If you didn't know any better, it would all seem almost to be some...vast bulwark of confusion and misdirection. There's hardly any...direct grasp, of anything. Everything's only ever somewhat like something else. "The image of an image, the symbol of an illusion." Now I'm sure that was Anatole France, wasn't it?

ML: I'm afraid I can't help you there.

FV: Of course, if you go back far enough, you'll arrive at a few archaic morphemes and phonemes, completely lost in origin and meaning, which may be, in some sense, unique... But then, you're left there with only the pure abstraction of a name - just a sound - lacking any inherent relationship to the thing being named, or to anything else...and is that any better?

ML: I don't know.

FV: Well, it's not important, I suppose. I'm just going off on a tangent here. Perhaps one in my business just sees too many words, too many times...sort of a *jamais vu* sets in, as they say.

ML: Deja vu?

FV: No, *jamais*, the opposite...'never saw'. When something familiar becomes unfamiliar...*uncanny*, as if you'd never really seen it before. And then there's the other one —

ML: There's another?

FV: *Presque vu*, or 'almost saw,' where you can't quite latch onto an idea...like a word on the tip of your tongue.

ML: Huh. I'd only ever heard of the one. Strange how the other two never became quite as popular in English. Do the French experience these sensations more often, or something?

FV: Like the Germans experience *schadenfreude*?

ML *[laughing]*: I guess.

FV: I couldn't say. But there, as you've seen, a translation of all these words can still be made...or, at least, a definition... A description of the *gist*.

ML: So it would seem.

FV: Then again, though, there is a certain power in the...singularity of a word - that "spell of a name" - which won't always come across...like the way your average English speaker will tend to view 'pink' as something of a distinct colour, in-and-of itself, as opposed to simply a particular shade of light red... Just as the Russian would differentiate between *goluboj* and *sinij* rather than associate a light blue with darker one...or so I'd assume, anyway. That whole linguistic relativity thing.

ML: Right. Like with the Eskimo - or Innuit, I should say - and his umpteen different words for snow.

FV: Yes...though that's possibly apocryphal, but yes.

And who's to say those umpteen hypothetical words don't actually identify umpteen different, and quite separate things, which we've just clumsily lumped together under the ignorant heading of 'snow'?

ML: I'm sure they'd know better than us.

FV: You'd think... But then, they might not. How much do we know ourselves of the *umptillion* variations and synonyms we have for various things? I mean...well, take, for instance, the words 'city' and 'town'...and 'village'. Now the Innuit may see these words only as we see his 'snow'. Or, at most, simply...units of size for what is essentially the same kind of thing. As might we, for that matter —

ML: As I would, myself.

FV: But, going back, they differ even further, on a much deeper level. If you'll indulge me - 'village', to start with, comes from the Latin *villaticum*, and so etymologically defines itself through...its physical construction, you might say...by relating to the buildings on a farmstead, or *villas*. 'City', however, derives from *civis*, and is thus defined more by its contents: the people, or *civilians*.

ML: I see.

FV: Then 'town', differing again, refers to...a separation from its surroundings, coming from an old Germanic word for a fence, or hedge...itself a borrowing from an older Celtic word, I believe, for 'fortress'.

ML: Interesting.

FV: Now compare these to, say...the Japanese *shi*, referring to a place of commerce, or...the Arabic *madina*, regarding obedience to a ruler. Then, of course, there's the German *stadt*, from a root meaning simply 'to stand', as opposed to our 'settlement' which, of course, concerns sitting. You see? None quite line-up, eye to eye. Nor, for that matter, do any of them, really, quite address themselves. It's all like Beckett's heap... What really is a 'town' or a 'city'...a *madina* or a *stadt*...in the overall, synonymic sense? And, if there is no common definition for such a thing, does such a thing actually exist? Is there only just a London and a Toronto...a Damascus and a Berlin?

ML: There should be some commonality there. They all share...well, let's see... I'd say they're...more-or-less permanent collections of people...in a certain place...with streets and buildings... Well, I guess those aren't absolutely necessary. But certainly people —

FV: Ah, but even here there is little agreement on just what 'people' actually are. I mean, are we 'men', heavenly descendents of the Indo-Germanic god *Manu*? Or are we 'humans', mere outgrowths of the *humus*, or 'earth'? Or, then, are we 'individuals' who, as the name suggests, are single, un-dividable beings? Or are we 'persons,' composed of both a body and an Etruscan *phersu*, or mask? The origin of 'people' itself is rather obscure, although, strangely, in Classical Latin *populatio* meant 'devastation'.

ML: I guess I don't really know what we are, then...

or where. But that's what dictionaries are for, I suppose.

FV: Indeed! For if words were in any way clear and self-evident - meaningful in themselves - then why should we ever have need of such things? Surely not just for spelling. Some would argue, in fact, that we only ever give the dictionary headwords - the *lemmata* - to things, and not any meaning at all...that there is, in the end, only semantics...terminology and denotation. That if you seek so-called "meaning" you need look no further than one of these...

[With this, Vanderson produced a tiny Collins Gem Dictionary *from somewhere on his person.]*

ML: Do you always carry a dictionary around with you?

FV: You can never be too careful.

ML: OK...

FV: It's actually quite handy to have around, aside from looking up words. The appendix has a list of weights and measures, conversion tables..."Quick Ways with Figures," if you need to calculate your prices in farthings and shillings —

ML: I see.

FV: I collect these, actually...dictionaries. It's an endlessly absorbing hobby - so many titles and editions, so many kinds...each with their own definitions and examples... And why should that be, do you suppose?

ML: I'm sure money must be one reason.

FV *[laughing]*: Well, of course...and much of it mine! But that aside, how is it that one word can have so many varied definitions? And why should some of these definitions - often of the shortest and simplest words - require the better part of a page, or more, to fully explain themselves? I mean, which really is the true barer of meaning, the word or the definition? - "many-worded name," as I believe John Mill had called it.

ML: Meaning, eh? Well...I'd have thought a word is sort of a short-hand version of the definition, or meaning...of a concept, really, I suppose. But then, even the definition is something of an...abbreviation, I guess, of the actual thing.

FV: An abbreviation, a condensation, yes...what programmers would call "data compression" as I've learned from translating more than a few IT communiqués over the years. But, as I've also learned, with any compression there is always some loss of information, or resolution...of *definition*, if you will. From the thing itself, to some concept of it, to a definition, and finally a word...it would seem to be degradation all the way down, wouldn't it?

ML: Well, if you take that analogy far enough —

FV: I can take it even further than that! If you've read any actual computer code...or, for that matter, any language theory...any philosophy or formal logic, written in any *formalized* way, with words and functions themselves reduced to mere algebraic notation; by..."letting P represent the predicate of... speech act X, wherein we assign...a truth-value T to Y, so that PXT equals QRS," or whatever nonsense.

ML: Ugh...I vaguely recall suffering through some of that stuff in school. Tended to make my brain glaze over.

FV: Likewise. Of course, it's all intended to simplify and clarify things...or, at least, to expedite them. But it would seem that whatever's saved during the input, or encoding process, is just taken back in the output...in the effort to decode, or decompile whatever's being said. Trying to remember what everything's supposed to stand for, then spelling it back out into some normal language in your head.

ML: Sort of a zero-sum game.

FV: At least for the reader...at least until he becomes accustomed to the short-hand and it gradually becomes a "normal language" itself. After that it would seem to all work fine - or, at least, fast. And wouldn't all the great treatises, or novels get written so much quicker if we'd just "let P represent the protagonist, and...$C2$ the conflict encountered in the second chapter with sub-character $X4$," et cetera?

ML: I somehow doubt that would catch on.

FV: No...not yet, anyhow. It seems there's still something to be said for description...elaboration —

ML: But I don't see how you could ever completely replace coding...or words - if that's what you're getting at - with just more elaboration..."many-worded names." I mean, they're just that, aren't they? Many-*worded*.

FV: Indeed! One can't exist without the other. In fact, it would seem one can't exist without an endless regress of the other, then the other, then the other... Sort of an inversion, in a way, of that old problem of learning a language from scratch from one of these books here. All the words are inside, but where do you begin?

ML: Right.

FV: And, for that matter, which dictionary should you use? Like I was saying, there's so many to choose from...and each with it's own peculiarities. Take an *Annandale*, which - and don't ask me how I remember this - defines 'definition' as "an explanation of the signification of a term." Yet *Oxford*, on the other hand, defines it as "a statement of the precise meaning of a word." A small, perhaps negligible difference you might think. And neither, would you say, is necessarily more correct than the other?

ML: I suppose not. No.

FV: But now look up each of the words comprising each definition, and then the definitions of those definitions, and so on. Some still may only differ slightly, while others may differ quite a lot. Yet any discrepancy, large or small, only compounds that initial difference further and further, pushing each 'definition' farther apart. How similar are they then at the end of this process...assuming it ever would end? Could we possibly even be referring to the same word by this point? And we still haven't considered what *Collins* here...or *Gage*, or *Funk and Wagnalls* might have to say about it. Off on enough tangents and you're eventually led completely off track.

ML: Or around in circles.

FV: Precisely!

ML: *Oxford*, though, is generally considered the authority, isn't it?

FV: Well, it's certainly the biggest...the most complete. But then, that truly is your vicious circle - every word defined...every word in every definition defined...around and around in an infinite loop. Truly a book that never ends. A concise, or abridged dictionary may, at least, have an out...some word in some definition which isn't itself defined. And perhaps, counter-intuitively, you could start there, somehow, to decipher the language —

ML: Like that little *Gem* you've got there?

FV: Perhaps. It's certainly small enough.

ML: I wonder, then, what the smallest possible "complete dictionary" would be? Completely self-contained, that is, with every word in every definition accounted for. How many would that be, do you suppose? Or, I guess more importantly, which ones?

FV: Well, that brings to mind another problem. You know that Russell riddle about the numbers?

ML: I don't think so.

FV: Or was it Berry who introduced it to Russell...or Jules Richard who introduced it to Berry...? Anyways, it's about identifying astronomically large numbers with astronomically long names...of ten, fifteen, or twenty syllables —

ML: So like...a *dodeca...quintillion...oogolplex*, or something?

FV: Right. And Russell, or Berry, posed the problem of citing the...now how does it go...? "The smallest number not nameable in less than twenty syllables." But, of course, just in saying this you've already cited the number with a "many-worded name" of only nineteen syllables. Thus, in effect, describing into existence something that shouldn't be able to exist!

ML: Hmm. Wait...that's eighteen...seventeen syllables, actually.

FV: Oh...? So it is. I suppose Berry phrased it another way. But then, you could phrase it even more succinctly than that, simply by referring to 'The Berry Paradox' or, perhaps, just 'Berry's Number'.

ML: Or just 'BN'.

FV: Or replace all linguistic and alphabetic coherence with some strange new symbol...assuming all the Greek letters have been taken by now. But then, it's still a kind of language however it's written.

And such is language's power that we speak into being things which cannot be...heaps, and liars, and strange numbers...all these paradoxes and contradictions... Strange, then, that 'contradiction' itself translates literally as 'against speech', or 'to speak against'.

ML: I must say, you seem somewhat inclined to speak against words yourself.

FV *[laughing]*: Well, what was it Frye also warned of? That..."cult of the wordless," chasing red herrings..."writing books by the score on the utter inadequacy of words." I wouldn't say I have anything against them... It's just...I don't know. Even before Frye, and getting into translation, I always had something of a strange relationship with language, I guess you could say.

ML: Strange? How so?

FV: Well...at one point, as a small child, for instance - I just remembered this, actually - I sort of...began to suspect that the words I had learned for certain things did not, in some way, seem to match what they claimed to represent. 'Water', I recall... something about that 'er' didn't quite sit with me... and that 't'...it didn't seem to belong where it was.

ML: Really?

FV: I went so far as to stare at a running faucet once, in the bathroom or kitchen. I must have stood there...I don't know how long...mouthing sounds as they came to me from...who knows where? Trying to glean from the water's...essence, I suppose, what its true name might be. I found myself, at last, deciding on something along the lines of "*dauna.*"

ML: Donna?

FV: The word seemed to fit for some reason. And, secretly, I even carried it along as a synonym for years, in a sort of personal thesaurus that I'd mentally compiled. Only later in life did I come to learn of the Indo-European word *danu*, meaning 'to flow'; where we get our names for the Danube, Dnieper, and Don...quite a few other watery things.

ML: That *is* strange!

FV: Well, I don't think I ever conjured up any other...what's the word? Nothing quite of the same coincidence. What's the word I'm looking for?

ML: I don't know. Perhaps there's a German word for it?

FV: No...well, probably, yes. If I can think of what it is I'm trying to... '*Phonesthesic*'! That's the word.

ML: *Gesundheit*!

FV *[laughing]*: Yes, well —

ML: So are you saying that there might be some hidden...proper language for things that we might have lost? Or —

FV: No, no, no. I don't have any...what would you call it? Nothing like that, anyway. I don't know...it's just, when you think about it all, sometimes, it just all seems a little...strange.

ML: I suppose.

FV: Actually, I really began having my suspicions around the time I started learning Chinese... I would teach myself by translating random passages from books, or newspaper articles, from one language to the other, and vice versa. This one time, though, there was a bit of English I was trying to work out... I can't seem to recall what it was now...but I got caught on the word 'something'.

ML: 'Something'?

FV: You see, the phrase-book I was using listed two options in Chinese - *mǒu shì*, which pertains to a task or an action, as in 'to do something', and...*mǒu wù*, pertaining to an object or substance, as in 'to be something'. But the way it was being used in English was the more generic, ambiguous...metaphysical sense, I guess. As in an unknown. Not necessarily an action, or an object, or anything, really...just, you know...*something*.

ML: OK.

FV: I then started looking into the *hanzi* themselves, trying to discern their own etymologies to see if one might be more appropriate than the other... The *shì* character, I found, seemed to depict what might be construed as a mouth giving orders next to a crop being planted. Very much 'to do something'. *Wù*, on the other hand, translates...or, transliterates as something like 'not a cow'.

ML: 'Not a cow'? That doesn't sound very helpful!

FV: No. But in Chinese that's sort of the general term for 'object'.

ML: That's certainly a strange way to define it.

FV: Well, cows were likely very important...very prevalent in ancient China. You might imagine there was sort of a "cows, and everything else" mentality. At least, that's what I'm guessing.

ML: I see.

FV: Anyways, then, both seemed very fixed in what they stood for. I wasn't any further along. I eventually consulted a Chinese colleague of mine...well, actually, the owner of my local convenience store —

ML *[laughing]*: OK.

FV: I tried to explain the kind of 'something' I had in mind, but he didn't seem to understand what I was trying to say. Admittedly, his English wasn't that good itself, but I started thinking...perhaps I didn't really know what I had in mind either. Or, perhaps the English word itself was somehow insufficient. I then looked into its own etymology and found 'thing' to be, originally, an assembly, or type of meeting, from Saxon days. It relates, in a sense, more to a period of time than either an object or an action. 'Some', meanwhile, shares a common root with 'similar' and 'same'...like an analogy. Whereas the Chinese counterpart *mǒu* seems more to denote specificity...a singling out; the pictogram representing a sweet tasting fruit, as if to signify a selection, or preference, as opposed to a comparison.

ML: So in English 'something' is '*like* an old Saxon meeting', where in Chinese it's either...'*this* order to plant crops' or...'*this*, which is not a cow'?

FV: So to speak.

ML: Like the burned-up saint I'm wearing as pants?

FV: Yes... But your pants, though...at least, no matter what you might call them, are there on your legs, for all to see. But where is the 'something'? Where is '*anything*' for that matter?

ML: I don't know. I'm not sure I understand what you're getting at.

FV: Well...let me ask you this. When is the last time you believe that you did understand something? That is, something you read, or that was said to you —

ML: The word 'something'?

FV: No, just...anything. Or —

ML: Oh, then...I guess, at the risk of sounding presumptuous, just now, I would think. At least mostly, anyhow...haven't I?

FV: OK. But allow me, just for a moment, to propose that you may actually not have understood that...or this...or anything that either you, or myself, have just said... Nor anything anyone else has ever said. In fact, let me put it to you that nothing which has ever been said has ever really been understood by anyone, because nothing which has ever been said has actually ever said anything!

ML: You don't say.

FV: Tell me, hasn't it ever struck you as somewhat... perverse that when trying approach a clearer description of...*some*thing we invariably...inevitably retreat backward, resorting to the 'some' of the thing? Some *similarity*? That when attempting to close the gap between a concept, and our understanding of it, we only, in effect, increase that distance through the use of metaphor, or... metonymy? Through comparison, or simile...an allusion, allegory, or analogy? Doesn't it seem that we only ever really refer...defer, and deflect... superficially relate all that is completely unrelated? Does the entire linguistic process not appear to be - at least, at *some* level - simply an elaborate system of avoiding the issue?

ML: Well..."all thinking is metaphorical," as I believe Robert Frost once said.

FV: Yes, and "to know is merely to work with one's favourite metaphors," as Hegel, or Nietzsche, or someone else said, too. But why? Why these words, made of metaphors; in descriptions, made of metaphors; composing stories, parables...more metaphors? Everything more and more removed... Look, I'm sure this all sounds a bit odd coming from a professional translator —

ML: A little.

FV: But the two things are actually quite intertwined - 'translation' and 'metaphor'. They are, in fact, merely Latin and Greek compounds meaning, at root, the same thing - that is, 'to carry' or 'carry over'. But...couldn't it just as easily mean 'to carry away'? To take it all further and further from whatever it truly is...whatever *it* is?

ML: I don't —

FV: You know, it's been said that the mind is somewhat...mis-calibrated. That it rarely, if ever, hits the mark in its analysis of things. Rather, it tends to skew either one of two ways...on the one hand, over-simplifying, generalizing, categorizing, and abstracting...as with words. Then, on the other, over-complicating things; making connections and finding patterns where there's none to be found... creating stories out of that which there's nothing to tell. And in metaphor...in language, wouldn't it seem we accomplish both these inaccuracies at once? I mean, perhaps that's its attraction. But then... perhaps, that's more of the cause... Listen, as a fellow man of letters, you're surely familiar with all the various theories regarding the extent to which language influences our thoughts?

ML: Well, not all of them.

FV: It was Saussure... No, it couldn't have been Saussure. Suessmilch, it must have been, who argued that *all* thought, in fact, stems from language. Still, though, he conceded the invention of language to be quite...*unthinkable* without the prior faculty of thought.

ML: That would seem to be a paradox.

FV: Yes, another paradox...another contradiction. An 'antinomy', you could also say. Not to be confused with the 'anti*mony*' that they use on certain printing plates...and in that old purgative pill that one could pass, or regurgitate, then use over again. But, I digress... Now, actually Vico, come to think of it, even before Suessmilch, traced 'logic's' Greek root *logos* to both 'idea' and 'word'...claiming at one point it was also entwined with the concept of *muthos*, or 'myth'. And Suessmilch, himself, circumvented his own particular antinomy by ascribing language to a gift from God.

ML: Works every time.

FV: Indeed...as you must also be aware that, long before the advent of philology, or semiotics, or...psycholinguistics, the concept of a *divine word* - one which brought with it human intelligence, enlightenment, even life itself - permeated nearly every culture on earth.

ML: I'm somewhat aware.

FV: To many Jews, of course, everything derives from the *Tetragrammaton* - the unspeakable name of God himself. While to Hindus, the sacred syllable *Om* is the very breath of existence. The Mayan universe was said to be spoken into being through a conversation between deities...and even the gods have been "called forth by name," as in Babylonian myth, or "spat from the mouth of Khepri" as in ancient Egypt... Then, of course, from the Greek god Hermes we get 'hermeneutics'...and from the Greek word for 'holy' we get 'hieroglyphics'. Did you know, also, that the Tibetan word for 'religion' is the same as that for 'book'? And our own word 'religion', for that matter, has been said to come from the Latin *relegare*, which means 'to read'...or 'read again'... *Iqra*, or 'read', in fact, was the first word Allah spoke to Muhammad in the cave, and —

ML: "In the beginning was the *Word*, and the *Word* was God."

FV: Exactly! And 'God' itself, you know, may descend from the ancient root *ghut*, meaning 'to call' or invoke. But just who, or what, is this 'God' we continue to call upon? You may recall the words of Miller...or Müller, wasn't it? The great Victorian orientalist and translator. He referred to religion as a "disease of language;" crude explanations rendered to myth by the constraint of words...words themselves reified into gods. But, I must confess, such distortions strike me more as the symptoms of an illness, rather than its cause. Couldn't it be that language itself is the disease?

ML: Is that your diagnosis?

FV: It's by no means a new one. Wasn't it Joseph Campbell...? No, it was Campbell quoting Jung - I'm quite sure - who claimed that all religion is merely a defence against true religious experience. For the real experience, you see, cannot be *told* to you by some priest, nor *read* in any book. And do you also remember your Plato? In *Phaedrus*...no, *Phaedo*...

Vanderson here went on to recount the episode in *Phaedrus* where Socrates tells of Thoth, the ibis-headed deity of ancient Egypt who bestowed writing upon the world, and how the god-king Amun, in turn, disparaged this new invention. Quoting and paraphrasing in equal parts, Vanderson retold the entire passage with a strange, theatric gusto. In closing he even assumed the role of Amun himself, raising his now empty tumbler for dramatic emphasis, and punctuating his performance with the king's final judgement...

FV: "This *potion* of yours will not give your disciples truth, only the semblance of truth! They will read many things while, in practice, learn nothing! They will display only the pretence of wisdom without ever acquiring its reality!"

ML: How many of those have you had?

FV: Ah, time for another already, is it? What will you have this round?

[I was still only halfway through my own gin buck when Vanderson ordered up another of his "potions." This time, a perplexing concoction of Yukon Jack and cream soda.]

ML: You have an adventurous taste in drinks, I'll give you that.

FV: Well, I come here a lot. You have to try something new, every once in a while... Keeps things interesting.

ML: Is there anything you haven't tried here yet?

FV: Oh, of course. The combinations are endless...

I'm sure I'll never get around to all of them - not that it'll stop my attempt! It's always good to try new things, though... Anyways, where were we at?

ML: I believe you were quoting Amun-Ra...or Socrates...or Plato, anyways.

FV: Ah... I do tend to do that, don't I? "Speak the words of a million dead souls before," to quote yet another dead soul...Hermann Bahr, I think.

ML: Oh, no. I do it all the time myself.

FV: It is all that much easier, isn't it?

ML: No need to re-state what's already been said so well.

FV: Quite so... In fact, what need is there to state anything of your own when everything's already, pretty well, been said? Why attempt any witticism when mere...*psittacism* will do?

ML *[laughing]*: Why indeed?

FV: Why, for that matter, bother to think for yourself when you can simply...take someone's *word* for it? Why even engage with life when one can merely engage in conversation? "We know the expression for every feeling before we ever feel it," as Bahr said too... "Hostages of a dead world."

ML: Well...that's a bit grim, isn't it?

FV: Is it, though? I'm not really sure... You know, I remember reading a paper once, on...*The Origin and*

Meaning of Language, or something like that. I wish I could remember the author...a Zildjian, or Zerzan...someone like that. But, in the span of about ten pages, he managed to quote or reference some fifty separate authorities on the matter, including himself! I mean...the way we recycle all the same thoughts and ideas...and then all in this language - the clichés that are words themselves - it's all very much like that antimony pill, isn't it? Just regurgitating the same commonplaces, down through time...only to be swallowed again by the next generation. And what is it we're actually saying, in the end, with these '*heaps*', and '*cities*', and '*somethings*'? It's almost as if, in a sense, we can only use words by not knowing what they actually say...only understand them by not knowing what they really mean. It's almost as if by this trick, this sleight, we've somehow invoked our own...figurative disengagement from the world itself - transported ourselves to a place where everything we speak of, if not meaning something else, means nothing at all... But, of course, I'm not saying anything you haven't already heard.

ML: No, listen...it's all very thought provoking stuff. A little out-there, perhaps —

FV: Perhaps...or perhaps not. It may not be such a crazy notion. The case has been made that language's initial purpose was, in fact, the prevention of knowledge...of truth - that all communication stems from a deep-seeded need to lie. There's another old quote...some French diplomat, I think, who said that language was given to man only so that he may "disguise his true thoughts."

ML: Not a surprising stance for a statesman to take.

FV: No, you're right there... Talleyrand, it must have been...to survive *Louis Seize*, the Revolution, Napoleon - up until the Second Republic, I think - he would surely have been proficient in the art of "disguise."

ML: You'd think for language to have survived all this time, though, truth must have entered in at some point... I mean, unless we're all some species of gullible —

FV: Well, if you believe the work of David Lewis... or was that Donald Davidson? - one of those analytics, anyway - the persistence of language is, indeed, a "convention of truthfulness," based solely on trust between speakers. And, after all, what point is there in communication if not to transmit and receive information that is useful...that's *true*?

ML: Right.

FV: Therefor, any society of liars - like those Cretans, I suppose - must truly be "a society of madman," as Lewis, or whoever it was, also said - each oblivious to one another's faithlessness in words. For what point is there in lying if you don't expect to be believed?

ML: What indeed?

FV: But then, if ours is a society of truth-tellers, trusting in a language that *is* based on a lie - or, perhaps, on nothing at all - wouldn't one who believed he spoke the truth also be more than a little bit mad? Might we not all, in this way, be a little insane? Would this whole conversation not just be some...deranged exercise in mental illness?

ML: Well —

FV: Let me put it this way: don't you find it odd that two of the foremost symptoms of insanity are the hearing voices and talking to oneself? Is it any wonder that language is an area of such interest in psychology? I think it was Otto Rank...or Thomas Szasz, who went so far as to claim that we, as humans, no longer even live in our own bodies at all, but in our language alone. Freud...perhaps even James, at least went as far as Talleyrand in agreeing that language serves more to conceal...to suppress the bare expressions and gestures of our more primal emotions...hide them all beneath a pile of words, as it were. And Lacan, I believe, questioned the very ability of anyone to ever tell the *actual* truth about anything - even if they wanted to...even if they could - given the limited scope of words themselves.

ML: You've done your research, I can't argue with that. And I thought you said that you hadn't been reading! Might I suggest, though, that you could simply be a little over worked? You really are beginning to sound as one who's seen a few too many words lately.

FV *[laughing]*: Maybe you're right. Look, I don't mean to go off with all this. You wanted to talk about translating, and —

ML: No, again, this is all interesting stuff. We can go

wherever you like...any topic you wish to broach.

FV: Even if the topics which language limits us to aren't much worth discussing in the first place?

ML *[laughing]*: Well, I find anything to do with language is generally worth discussing.

FV: Yes, but discussions on the failures of language, through the use of language...its always something of a sleeveless errand.

ML: But entertaining, nonetheless.

FV: So you still wish to be entertained by my ramblings, then?

ML: I think, by now, that should go without saying.

FV: Alright... Well, then perhaps it *should* go without saying. Perhaps it *all* should! For isn't one of the first lessons of good elocution that there's nothing one can say in any rambling, sprawling rant that can't, through some effort, be said shorter and better with a little careful editing?

ML: Yes.

FV: Or that, in writing, there's nothing you can describe in any page-filling paragraph that can't be captured better in just a sentence or two? Perhaps even nothing in any sentence which cannot better be refined in a single, spot-on word?

ML: Well, "brevity is the soul of wit."

FV: Does it not follow, then, that there's likely nothing one can say in any word - in saying anything at all - that, ultimately, isn't better left unsaid? Does it not simply imply that there is really nothing, in the end, that anyone can say?

ML: So...did you want to end the interview, then? Or —

FV: Oh, I'm just getting started again! In fact, lets start right from the beginning...get right back to translation.

ML: Alright.

FV: You know, I once had to translate a piece of braille, not long ago...some "workplace accessibility" something-or-other. Now, talk about losing information - for all the connotations that a word might conjure-up mentally, in braille there is, of course, a whole physical experience that is also lost in the process! But, that aside, you know many of the great writers were themselves blind...Homer, Milton, Al-Maʿarri, Borges... In many African cultures, in fact, it was customary to blind the tribal storyteller on purpose... And the old Slavic word *sliepac*, come to think of it, meant both 'blind' and 'bard'. But why do you think that should be?

ML: I don't know.

FV: Doesn't that old parable of the blind men trying to describe an elephant come to mind? You know the one - each of them feeling a separate part, but none with a proper conception of the animal as a whole. And isn't any writer...any commentator or chronicler something like this? Aren't we all, in a way, not only blind to the meaning of own words, but, well... You questioned earlier how I seek only the *gist* from translations?

ML: Yes.

FV: Well, tell me, what is lost in that initial *translation* between our mind and our senses...the whole world around us? We know there are colours in the spectrum *untranslatable* to our eyes; sounds beyond the range of our hearing; sensations beyond the tolerance of taste or touch. What else is there that we might be missing? Could it be that we, ourselves, only ever really experience the mere *gist* of our own lives?

ML: I suppose so.

FV: Well, if you really do suppose, you should begin to realize how infinitely more unspeakable...how completely absurd that subsequent translation, between a thought or experience into any vocabulary, really is...and then, how preposterous the task of further rendering into other tongues such futile expressions, which says so little to begin with, truly becomes... And particularly when they culminate in this - the most perfidious...most insidious tongue of them all - English! This most mongrelised, most bastardised, most globalised language; this confused muddle of loans and derivations, borrowings and re-borrowings, so divorced from any source or meaning as to surely be utter nonsense!

ML: Well, I'm afraid I don't speak any other tongues.

Or, any...*non-tongues*, for that matter. Perhaps you'd prefer we continue through...what? An exchange of sketches, or...interpretive dance?

FV *[laughing]*: No, my dancing days are far behind me... Anyways, there, of course, you're just replacing some vocal form of speech with a gestural one. An un-standardised sign language, if you will...blindness exchanged for deafness. And drawing...well, how much different from writing is that? Are words not simply "the pictures of thought," as Aleister...no, not Aleister Crowley - good Lord! Who was that...? *Abraham Cowley*, that's it! "Words, but the pictures of thought...though we our thoughts from them perversely draw." And, indeed, 'drawing' itself is *drawn* from 'draw'.

ML: The word?

FV: Related to 'drag', from the old Germanic *draganan*, which, like 'translate' and 'metaphor', means 'to carry'. And, so it is, that perversion of similarity continues on down through the alphabet itself - that anachronistic symbology of...stylised bull heads, and whatever else all those other letters were originally meant to represent.

ML: Ah, that's right. They were all, more-or-less, pictographic, or...hieroglyphic to begin with, weren't they?

FV: But, see, now you're going to get me started on the whole business of graphemes and orthography... transliteration...allography, and all of its complications!

ML: I just meant that a drawing, or picture, I guess... Well, each is worth a thousand words, as they say.

FV: That is what they say, isn't it? But then, if words truly are as meaningless as we might suspect, a thousand noughts still amounts to nothing...no?

ML: OK, but putting words aside... Or, are you trying to suggest now that any form of communication is futile?

FV: Surely not! How would one even express such a thing?

ML *[laughing]*: Well, you tell me.

FV: I don't know... Perhaps there's some mathematical principle to it all. That adage you used is somewhat telling in itself - how we seem so fond of assigning "worth" and values to everything... grouping into classes and sets...then calculating... equating it all through these metaphoric functions of ours. Has a picture any value beyond words, or vice versa, if we only ever think in language? This speaks, also, to a certain...conceit of rigour, that we should take such a mathematical approach to our forms of expression; the confining of...transitory experience, or reverie, to material dimensions... As if an exact *equation* of words...the precise *formula* of colours, images, or sounds might somehow evoke, or reproduce, the correct semblance of...whatever.

ML: You did liken yourself to a mathematician, though, didn't you? Or, said that translation is...or, at least, *should* be mathematical.

FV: Well, as opposed to artistic, yes...if one can really make that distinction. Of course, Frye, again, likened literature - all writing - to mathematics, I think... Just as Gauss once referred to math as "a kind of poetry." Or was that Weierstrass? At any rate, from what I've been saying, perhaps I, myself, have been taking the wrong approach. After all, what should it matter how one line of gibberish adds up to another? I think I may have simply acquired something of an aversion to "art" itself, over the years. And then, once you start talking of drawings and dance —

ML: What is it against art that you have?

FV: Well...it just so often seems the lowest type of expression. But, as I've said, I tend to prefer things a little more straight-ahead. Probably because artistic writing itself is so damned hard to translate...what with all those subtleties and intangibles. And then, just, you know...there's all of the affect and pretension that can go along with it. I find it hard to take serious anything subject to the whims of fashion, or style, you know? I suppose that's why I find it hard to take much of anything seriously these days.

ML: As a "mathematician," then, you don't have to worry so much about, say...2 and 2 making 4, going out of style?

FV: I guess not. But...I'm not really sure that you're even safe there. When I was first learning long division, you know - way back in prehistory - I recall being taught that any number divided by zero remained unchanged. Later, however, I was told that such a quotient could equal either the dividend or the divisor. By the time I reached highschool, I believe, the answer became "undefined"...even "meaningless." Then, when I began calculus, I was instructed that it might, in fact, represent infinity! Now, how do you explain that?

ML: Well...math was never exactly one of my strong suits.

FV: Nor mine, believe me! But it's an interesting subject to read up on. I've since learned, in fact, that the very concept of zero has been in and out of style a number of times. Infinity, too - even today - might seem quite *passé* in one "scene," if you will, while in another it may be very much *en vogue*...so much so that it can proliferate itself in an infinite variety of sub-styles, with ordinal infinities, cardinal infinities, transfinite infinities... At the same time, though, there's still many so-called "primitive" peoples who'll make no use of any digits which outnumber their fingers. And, in certain so-called "advanced" fields of modern math, there are those who'll profess to have no use for, say...negative numbers, or, perhaps, the irrationals. Then, there are cultures that have completely separate numbering systems for different kinds of objects...just as we have entirely different kinds of mathematics when dealing, for example, with the "continuum hypothesis" - which, itself, comes as a result of having too many of those infinities.

ML: I'm not terribly well versed in the "continuum hypothesis," I'm afraid...or much else of what you're talking about. I would think, however, that such things don't come about simply through the...

arbitrary vacillations of taste.

FV: You *would* think so, wouldn't you? And, perhaps, its not merely a matter of fashion. But the arbitrariness of the situation - now that you bring it up...I must say, I do find most, if not all things - once you inspect them closely enough - to be somewhat arbitrary in their design. At least, that's how they often appear to me... But then, as Charles...or Chester Fort would tell you, "there are no ways, except arbitrary ways, of judging anything." All opinions and appraisals, all estimations... qualifications and quantifications —

ML: I'm pretty that was *Charles* Fort, the paranormal...paradoxographer, right?

FV: Charles it is, then! But look here, at all these obscure measures in the back of my dictionary... Ten *deciares* to an *are*...half a *furlong* to a *hectometre*... *Firkins*, *kildirkens*, and *puncheons*... Twenty-one-and-a-half *quires* in a *printer's ream*. No accident, I'm sure, that Thoth was also god of calculation and measurement. Like writing, this too was all born of accounting and bureaucracy...from the need to weigh figs, count goats...parcel land. And, just as with words, it all remains inscrutably abstruse... ambiguous and vague. I mean, how much more definite is an 'inch', or a 'pound', than a 'heap' do you figure? What really is a 'metre'? A hundred 'centimetres'? Which are what? The hundredths of a 'metre'... Or, of course, they can be the sum of ten 'millimetres'...or one tenth of a 'decimetre' - which is what?

ML: Hardly used, for one thing...like those other

vu's you mentioned. Why is that, I wonder?

FV: I couldn't tell you. But a 'decimetre' is also ten 'centimetres'...and a hundred 'millimetres'...one ten thousandth of a 'kilometre'...about...one ninth of a 'yard'...or...3, or 4 'inches'... Twenty six "*whatevers*," 457.8 "*whatnots*"...five seventy-sixths of a "*so forth*," and an endless amount of infinitely lesser used conversions. All units of measurement, you see, are ultimately arbitrary...apparitions, defined only by their own ghostly reflections...'cities', 'towns', and 'villages'. Anything you try to quantify can be divided into any number of "*anythings*," or become the thing - the unit - itself. And what is any number, itself, but just another unit of measurement? What is a 'six' but two 'threes', or three 'twos'...half a 'twelve', or just six '*ones*' - which are what?

ML: The base units?

FV: So it would seem... But it also seems a shaky base on which to build a science, don't you think? Let me ask you this: when multiplying a number with itself, aren't you generally bound to get a greater total than if you merely add?

ML: Let's see... I think so, yes.

FV: Well then, how is it that when you perform this same operation with the number 'one' - the "base unit," or...*root morpheme* of this entire language - how is it, then, that in this case the exact opposite is true? 'One' multiplied by itself remains 'one', yet 'one' added to itself becomes 'two'! Is this not strange? Stranger still that 'two', when either multiplied or added with itself, produces an equal total! In this respect it shares the same properties of 'zero'! From its very foundations, then, the whole business of math seemingly doesn't add up...or at least, within only a few steps, adds up to nothing!

ML: *QED*?

FV *[laughing]*: It's a working hypothesis...I haven't fully fleshed it out yet. Still, I have to believe that numbers are only as real - or fictional - as any other words. Simply fabrications of ours, abstracted from this mad human urge to name. "Man is the measure of all things," after all - or, at least, as claimed by Pythagoras...or was it Protagoras? One of the two... Surely, though, in the *realest* sense, there's not actually any 'ones' or 'twos'...or 'twentys' out there...not *really*, do you think? Surely this is only possible through the vague generalizations of language...only where one simplifies to over-complicate, and the other way around. Truly, how can one ever discern a similarity, a metaphor between any *this* and any *that*, so precise as to actually make 'two' of a thing, let alone any more? And then, how does one discriminate, and divide between things...define their limits so as to begin counting - or naming - in the first place?

ML: It's an interesting theory...if I understand it right. But I'm afraid I'm going to need a little stronger proof than all that to go along with you.

FV: Oh, and I could readily supply you with one! But, of course, to go along all the way, any proof requires a proof itself...then a proof of the proof of the proof, and then...*quod erat demonstrandum, et cetera, ad infinitum*. In this way, all true proofs...all explanations, descriptions and definitions, must forever remain impenetrable...eternally unattainable ...lost within that dimension through which the infinity contained in everything extends.

ML: Dimension?

FV: Oh, like...when you take a line, for instance, and divide it...then divide the divided bits, and so on...each segment getting smaller and smaller... But mathematically, or theoretically, you can go on doing this, indefinitely, right?

ML: OK.

FV: But then - at least as the current *fashion* dictates - the "law of limits," or whatever it is, ensures that even an infinite number of progressively smaller lines will always add up to that original finite length, whatever it was...in the first dimension anyway. Yet...there's still an infinity of *something*, right? So where does that go? It must extend somewhere, toward something...right?

ML: A point?

FV: Perhaps...I don't know. I've confused myself now.

This talk of points, and lines, and various odd perspectives inevitably steered the conversation back to the topic of art, and Vanderson's apparent lack of use for it. Then came another break in the dialogue to lubricate once more. For my part, I was still sticking with gin - but now, taking Vanderson's lead, I decided to get a bit adventurous, switching out my ginger ale in favour of his chinotto (as a quinine-based drink, I figured it should come close enough to tonic as not to get *too* adventurous). Then Vanderson, in turn, partly took after me - albeit with sloe gin in his case, and then, even more divergently, mixing it with an English perry! After this we resumed our talk of art, which Vanderson - disapproving as he mostly was of it - seemed, nonetheless, quite well-versed in.

ML: You know, you remind me a bit of Huxley here...during one of his mescalin experiments, didn't he become a bit wary of art at one point, too? Something about how both language and art should be left to the "beginners and dead-enders"...or something to that effect. Laughing at a Gauguin, or Cézanne, and asking "who does he think he is?" over, and over —

FV: Are you suggesting I've been taking drugs?

ML *[laughing]*: I don't know. What else is in that drink?

FV: Nothing quite that strong...just strong enough. Perhaps I could stand to take a more sober view of the matter, though.

ML: But then, of course, wasn't it Baudelaire's...or Verlaine's prescription that "one must always be drunk, whether by wine or by art"?

FV: But then, didn't both of them die syphilitic lushes...wasted away on absinthe and laudanum, or whatnot?

ML: Ah, but didn't they all back then?

FV *[laughing]*: Those were, indeed, the days... But it is a similar effect which the two things produce, isn't it? McLuhan also, I think, made this comparison... and Freud, too, referred to art as a drug...or, rather, a "transient distraction, which induces a mild narcosis."

ML: Well, he preferred cocaine, didn't he?

FV: Six of one, half-a-dozen grams of the other. Perhaps there's really no difference at all. It all deals in escape and illusions...altered states.

ML: I can certainly speak to its addictive qualities... art, that is.

FV: Yes, it can become quite consuming as well. But then, if it really is like a drug, shouldn't one also worry about the potential side-effects?

ML: Such as?

FV: Could it be that, like a drug, art merely lures one into a false sense of something profound...where, in fact, it's simply making the abuser stupider, killing brain cells, so that things only *appear* as interesting as they do?

ML: That doesn't seem like my experience with it...with these drinks, perhaps. Do you really find yourself stupider after...hearing a great symphony, or viewing a great painting, or sculpture?

FV: I do get the sense from certain, more

contemporary works that I'm being made to feel stupid.

ML: Well, yes...that can happen.

FV: And the prices some of those things go for...the artists must already assume we're all a little dim... But, then, enough of us usually are. How much did the National Gallery pay for that Rothko, or Newman...that *stripe*, anyway? Almost $2 million, wasn't it? How else do you explain that, other than intoxication...or brain damage?

ML *[laughing]*: But that was, what?...10 years ago. They could probably sell it for twice as much now!

FV: So it's not about the amount of words a picture's worth, just the amount of cash?

ML: Sometimes, I'm sure. Not always, though...not usually.

FV: No...only in the most practical, honest cases. For if it's not an economic transaction, it's simply a...base exchange of worthless pretension for...abject attention. A...*sycophantic symbiosis* of...mutual false-validation, where a pandering artist attempts to procure praise and accolades from an audience hoping, in return, to...*osmose* from the art whichever perceived attributes fuel their artificial sense of superiority over those not yet in on the scheme.

ML: That's a bit cynical, isn't it?

FV: Is it?

ML: Of course that occurs, but...I wouldn't say any "art" made solely for those reasons is really *art* at all.

FV: No? Well, perhaps we're speaking of different things. Maybe we should define our terms... What has *Collins* to say? Let's see...here... 'Art', *noun*, "human skill as opposed to nature; skill applied to music, painting, poetry, et cetera; a system of rules...profession, craft."

ML: OK —

FV: Oh, this one's interesting: "a contrivance, cunning, or trick."

ML: Hold on - you're playing with a loaded dictionary!

FV *[laughing]*: No, look here...

ML: Alright. But those are only definitions, after all. "Meaningless words," remember?

FV: Quite so! Yet...hasn't all art, in a way, submitted to words - reduced itself to the literary...admitted its failure through all the catalogues and criticism... monographs and manifestos —

ML: Explanations?

FV: Exactly. All the *artistry*, now, seems expended in the rhetoric and sophistry used to differentiate...to justify its own existence now that so little is left to do. And who's to say how much of it ever needed doing in the first place?

ML: But who's to say it didn't?

FV: Oh, no-one, I suppose. It's just...well, representation has always been somewhat obsolete, hasn't it? "Realism," of any kind, has surely always been irrelevant in the face of reality itself...whereas the *depiction* of fantasy must naturally be inferior to the *experience* thereof. It all really amounts to mere fiction, or journalism...stories for those unable, or unwilling to confront the actuality themselves. And then, as for abstraction and..."conception" - it's all pretty much been abstracted and conceptualised to its logical ends. Nothing's been done here but the *re-writing* of rules, in denial that the game was already won, long ago, by the likes of Duchamp, Arp, or... Malevich. I mean, what's more...or, what's *less* to be said than a single black square?

ML: Well...a triangle has fewer sides, I suppose.

FV: Then a circle, a line, a dot... The rest is academic...obvious variations on an unnecessary theme, until you're left with just an empty canvas - which I'm sure has been done, too.

ML: Franz Kline, wasn't it...? Or, Yves Klein - didn't he once exhibit a completely empty gallery? No canvases at all.

FV: I guess, from there, to not exhibit anything - to do absolutely nothing at all - would be the next "conceptual" act...the ultimate multimedia performance, where all artforms converge in negation and silence. And someone's probably already put their signature to that, as well. But even this should be too much...to involve an artist, a name. Surely nothing, done by no-one, is the greatest possible artistic achievement. Yet, that too has been done...long, long ago. Before the very first artists ever walked the earth.

ML: True enough. But this is seeing art only through the lens of novelty, and...*fashion*, isn't it? What of art for art's sake...as expression, or elucidation...like we started off talking about?

FV: As a replacement for language?

ML: Perhaps.

FV: I'm afraid I can't see it. I mean, where language, at least, attempts to be specific in its meaninglessness, from art there never seems anything beyond...vague evocation, or...blunt sentimentality... I don't know, maybe that's just me. Perhaps I simply have a "high tolerance"... Of course, these days, the communication rarely ever lies in the work of art itself, anyway, does it? Only in the act of making it. "The medium is message," after all, right? But what's ever being said there, other than: "Hey, look at me!"?

ML: Well, it doesn't, necessarily, even need to involve communication, *per se*. Wasn't the whole goal of the minimalists - like Newman, *et al.* - to do away with all such expression and personality...to convey nothing but the *thing* in itself?

FV: OK...but again, why? What do I care about that "thing"...that surface or colour, that note or...stripe? And why do I need it presented by them, when there's already so many truly impersonal, monotonous *things* in the world to contemplate - without artists, and their...pedantic philosophies behind them, superseding and making superfluous the *thing* itself...whatever it is?

ML: I'm getting the sense that you must have some rather bare walls in your home.

FV *[laughing]*: Oh no...that would be far too "minimal" for my tastes. I can appreciate *some* decoration. I did - or, do, in fact - own two paintings ...or prints, rather. One a Duchamp, actually - his *Dulcinea*. Hung next to it was one of Monticelli's *Quixotes*. A fitting compliment, or pair, I thought...at the time.

ML: But you no longer have them up?

FV: No, they're still up...just behind a pair of bookshelves now. I would have moved them, or taken them down, but I have no other space to put them.

ML: So words truly did win over images?

FV: Just one affectation concealing another, really... The outer edges of the shelves, in fact, have been gradually filling-up with various items of clutter and *bric-à-brac*...a growing collection bottles, mostly. I find they have a certain aesthetic charm... Soon the books, too, will be hidden away.

ML: Then you have little need of words or images - symbols of any kind?

FV: Of course there's a need...or, an impulse. An inclination, at least. We're talking, aren't we? About art, no less. But its effect, or *affect*...its purpose, I guess, is still what troubles me. "We never arrive at anything but images and words...and so we won't die from the truth." This is what Schopenhauer said...or was that Nietzsche, too? But what "truth," I wonder? Perhaps if I could remember the whole quote... Still, how true could this "truth" even be, if it was arrived at by images and words itself?

ML: Another contradiction?

FV: Perhaps...though I do find something intriguing in that definition before. Just as 'contradictions' rise "against speech," isn't it strange how 'art' - and I'll include language in that - is "opposed to nature?" I sense there maybe is something *unnatural* about it all... Hasn't Jung also taught us that a word or image...a *symbol* "merely stands in for what cannot be thought?" But then, how do we ever think, but in symbols and words...meaningless in themselves, yet purporting to represent some kind of meaning? Are they truly *representations* of the things we wish to say? Or, are they more akin to *rituals*...ceremony - like the turning of a prayer wheel, or the laying of flowers at a grave - standing in for the things we cannot say...or the things for which there is nothing, really, to be said?

ML: I suppose you could be right.

FV: About what?

ML *[laughing]*: I don't know... I guess...well, "the truest ideas," didn't Barthes...or Bourdieu say?

"Need no words...ask for nothing but complicit silence." Something like that?

FV: There does seem a note of truth there, somewhere... A shame, then, he had to go ahead and say it.

ML *[laughing]*: Yes.

FV: But then, wasn't it Lao Tzu, or Laozi...or was it Lieh Tzu who said that, "with great wit comes great hypocrisy?"

ML: If you say so. I can only imagine... Such a burden, it must be, to have something great to express, and no good way to express it.

FV: Indeed. Still, you'd think that any truly wise notion would require no validation, as such...no audience to learn it...to approve, or reject it. Should the truth not be, after all, self-evident? Need only be acted upon, and communicated to no-one...exist only in itself...in "silence?" Doesn't the desire to *express* anything speak only of...insecurity and doubt? Of "truth" betrayed? Veiled questions in the guise of answers? The expression of any thought, you would think, might only be it's lowest form.

ML: So the truth, not only doesn't need to be communicated, but is...in some way, incommunicable?

FV: Well, if it *can* be told I'm sure I haven't heard it... It may be that the acts of a true sage will always go unnoticed, while only the *works* of artists, and the *words* of...hack aphorists echo on through time.

ML: Through people like us?

FV *[laughing]*: It seems to be working, doesn't it? Though...at least through quotation, and reference, we avoid all the egotism and...camouflage of that initial expression. Perhaps ours is a more honest betrayal of the "truth."

ML: Actually, I think I may be running a bit dry of quotations at this point.

FV: Well...then let us run all the way out! Perhaps, when one finally runs dry of *all* quotations - all references...connections, and influence - only then can he see the light. Perhaps truth must be unconditionally personal; an eternal secret...the one truly untranslatable thing... In a way, the grandest lie of them all...not only unbelievable, but... inconceivable... At least, to anyone except oneself.

ML: Then maybe its just a lie, period? No "truth," or "meaning," or any such thing. Just a random sequence of inconsequential events.

FV: Perhaps...but even that is a "truth" in itself, is it not? The question is - if such a thing can be articulated, can it also be true? Even when processed within yourself...is this still not just so much small talk...mere banter? Just another voice in the habit of filling silence with the coarse noise of its own... tedious inanity.

ML: Should it all, then, come in a flash? In an instant of...Zen enlightenment, or something?

FV: In a flash beyond Zen, I should think...I should hope. Not that I know much about the subject, however. Only the...who was it? "Baby monks," wasn't it?

ML: The who?

FV: Oh, another something I picked up while learning Chinese. It was this Buddhist sect, founded centuries ago...allegedly by a stillborn foetus; discovered by some monks in the woods near their temple.

ML: Really?

FV: So they say. And apparently this patron was held in the highest esteem, as no other school could claim lineage from a teacher so...assuredly absent of "self" and "mind"...as such Zen types are keen to avoid.

ML: I would guess not!

FV: Anyways, as the sect's fame grew, pilgrims began to come from all around to gain this... *mindless* wisdom. But, what do you suppose they actually got?

ML: I don't know.

FV: Well, one pilgrim, after asking a priest about "Buddha nature," or whatnot, was run through with a sword - killed on the spot! Another, asking who the "true Bodhidharma" might be, was imprisoned and tortured for several years...eventually cannibalized alive by the whole of the clergy.

ML: These were Buddhists?!

FV: Ultimately the entire school extinguished itself in a bloodbath of similar "enlightenments." Their authority was then usurped by a rival sect who followed the teachings of a stick.

ML: So...these monks, then...they were attempting to impart their wisdom through...experience? Is that it? Or were they just trying to withhold it?

FV: Or, were they simply cooped-up in their temple too long?

ML: They hadn't any wisdom at all, then?

FV: Who can say?

ML: Well, if the wise man...the "true sage," as you contend, always goes unnoticed...remains unknown ...that does beg a question —

FV: Yes..."if a tree falls in the forest," right? Well, what can I tell you? I've clearly said too much as it is. But...perhaps the silence, out there, speaks for itself. Maybe it is all a lie...that we've only invented the idea of "wise men" and *wisdom*...of knowledge, or "truth." *Verum factum*, after all, as Vico said... "man understands only what he himself has made." Yet, what can one make from such...scant materials as we posses - so finite in both our pursuits and capacities - this life and logic of ours, where any explanations we might ever have lay...lost in the eternal midst of endless, further inquiry? Every answer only begs another question...and just as Fort again...or maybe it *was* Crowley this time who proclaimed that "nothing has ever settled anything, except in the desire for settlement." That we "give up on *explanation*, and content ourselves only with *expressing*."

ML: A fate not even the most "mindless" can avoid?

FV: Not any who'd have "schools" and "teachings" ...or "wisdom." And, perhaps, just as those Zen *koans* of falling trees and clapping hands speciously employ the logic of language to...invoke some counter-logical sentiment, any understanding may work just the same...only played in reverse... All the same process, all towards the same empty result.

ML: I'm afraid you've lost me again.

FV: Well, it's... No... I've lost it myself, now.

This moment of uncertainty allowed for what, I assume, was a much needed bathroom break (I can't recall what number drink I was on at this point, nor if I had a chance to visit the men's room at any point prior). In my leave I had left the recorder running, needlessly draining power and space, capturing only Vanderson's silence as he re-gathered his thoughts. In hindsight, though, this may have been fortunate, as, in my state, if I had turned it off I likely wouldn't have remembered to switch it back on again.

Upon returning minutes later, with new space of my own to fill, I must have decided that one of Vanderson's strange blends might aid in following his increasingly strange discursions. To that presumed end, starting the next round, I asked for whatever he was having - and ended up with a Screech and Imperial sherry. As unpleasant a combination as this surely was, it, perhaps, now seemed a little tame on the heels of cannibalism...

FV: I guess, perhaps, what those monks were trying to get at is how it all may be such pointless violence.

ML: How what could?

FV: All of it...explanation, expression...even thinking, itself... Maybe knowledge, and its seeking, could be the root of it all? Perhaps it cannot be given, or received, because we already have it - we're already infected... Because to *understand* is to *already know*, and what is known is obvious... familiar, mundane - and what is mundane becomes tedious...oppressive...a burden; something to be repressed...to be forgotten, or fought.

ML: The truth is tedious?

FV: Well, wouldn't it be? An intolerable nuissance, once known long enough...a tired and worn-out trend? And would we not then, at some point, fashion the *untrue* - our "thoughts" - against it, in this constant pursuit of novelty and...*fashion*? Might any "advancements" and "progress" in knowledge, beyond what we had at the dawn of humanity, not only be reactionary flights from this tedium... contrarian escapes from the boredom of truth?

ML: And we just "already know" this "truth"... whatever it is?

FV: Well, the alternative is to learn...and how can one ever do that? How does one begin to know something without first understanding it? How does one understand without already knowing? If one must, in fact, learn...how does one learn to "learn?"

ML: There are instincts, I suppose —

FV: But what are *those*? Some physical process...a genetic program, or code - then subject to translation, degradation, and loss? And then, if Szilard...or Turing...or Heisenberg was right, if understanding, too, is a physical process... knowledge, itself, a physical substance - bound by physical laws...gained in one area only at the expense of another...subject to entropy and decay, beyond all its subsequent interpretations - it would seem, one can never leave this world with any more faculty than what one entered with. In fact, one *must* leave with less... Any knowledge beyond our initial capacity must always remain withheld, and what little we may possess slowly dwindles away...with every thought and reckoning... Even if there is no "learning," simply just some...*recollection* of things - a sudden regaining of that obvious knowledge... *anamnesis*, as Plato, or Socrates, would have it —

ML: From the man who said that he knew only that he knew nothing?

FV: That I said, or him?

ML: Didn't Socrates say that, too?

FV: He did, indeed... And, perhaps, these were the most sincere words to have ever been uttered...or, at least, to have been put in someone's mouth for them... But, then again, it could have just been wishful thinking.

ML: To know nothing?

FV: To know of knowing, perhaps. To be so self-aware... To not know what this "knowledge" really is...what this "truth" is all about. What are these things...really?

ML: You could try looking them up, as well.

FV: It's worth a shot... Alright then, here...
'knowledge' - "knowing; what one knows,"...OK. And, as for *'truth'*...well! "See 'true'." So, then, one is...circular tautology, and the other isn't even itself!

ML: We may need to start consulting a bigger dictionary.

FV: Oh, it wouldn't matter much. It's always the same linguistic run-around...always the same logical round-about. These circuitous words and circuitous thoughts...this game spent wandering in dark, desperate turns...groping blindly through labyrinths of our own creation...madly seeking clues to some non-existent mystery...consumed in intellect - this human life of ours - perhaps the lowest way to live.

ML: I have to say, you're beginning to depress me a bit. I'm usually more of a happy drunk. Would you really wish for another way of life? To be another *form* of life?

FV: I don't know... You've never pined as, who was it...Alcman...Alcaeus? To become as a halcyon...a "ceryl-bird?" To soar carelessly over everything... and just shit on it all?

ML: To become a bird-brain?

FV: *[laughing]*: Yes! Might it be, after all, that things really aren't so complicated? Not too complex to be reckoned with, but simply...too *simple*? Too "obvious?" Might it be that our brains are entirely over-qualified...that it all defies thinking, contemplation...reflection, or meditation? That any of our human contrivances toward understanding are just too clever for their own good? And, if so, wouldn't you then gladly give up all your human years for the brief, but...gloriously incognisant life of a bird?

ML: Well...you wouldn't, necessarily, even have to give up the lifespan. One of my aunts, you know, she had a parrot...or macaw, that lived over seventy years. Outlived her, in fact.

FV: That's true!

ML: It could even talk. She taught it to say —

FV: Bah! Now you've ruined it for me.

ML: Ah, sorry... But, at least, of course, they don't understand what they're saying.

FV: And we do? I think we've been over this.

ML *[laughing]*: Right.

FV: I can't bare to imagine the ridiculous life of a talking parrot...of inescapable, literal *psittacism*... Well, perhaps I can... In any event, though, I guess the bulk of most birds' lives is consumed with all that tweeting and squawking...*singing*. I suppose I'd have to go down the evolutionary ladder a ways to avoid this incessant chatter - to a lizard, or bug... maybe even a plant. Something that a bird would probably eat. But, then...why stop there? If I want to really get dumb, why not an amoeba, or...some kind of bacteria, or virus?

ML: I'm not sure if those are technically even life-forms.

FV: Bacteria are, I think...part of a "kingdom," or "phylum," at least, aren't they? For whatever that's worth... *Protistas...protozoa...prokaryotes...* something?

ML: You're asking the wrong guy.

FV: Perhaps a virus isn't, though. But...they move around, and multiply, don't they? They have no cells, however...isn't that it? But, then...is a sperm cell "alive?" I've often wondered that. It can create life... Ahh, let's see again... *'Life'* - "active principle of existence in animals and plants...animate existence, time of its lasting...history of such existence, way of living." Well, its not really an animal or plant...but, then, neither is a fungus —

ML: Would you really rather be a virus, or sperm cell?

FV: It doesn't seem like it would be much fun, does it? Well...I don't know. Perhaps it's not just a case of being too smart. It could be, after all, that we...or, at least, *I'm* simply not smart enough. Smart enough only to know I'm a fool.

ML: I'm not sure how much smarter you could be -
as a human, anyway...barring some unknown form
of alien intelligence.

FV: Well...we may not need to look off the planet for
that. I think an elephant's brain, if I'm not mistaken,
is about four or five times the size of our's...
Actually, I believe the blue...no, the *sperm* whale, in
fact, has the largest brain of any animal - some seven
times bigger!

ML: Is that so?

FV: We might be edged out by a few types of
dolphins, too... I think I've heard that our brains are
roughly the same size as a walrus'. Of course, there's
also something to do with...the brain's size in
relation to the rest of the body. In regulating all that
mass. I don't think it all goes to intelligence. But,
then, some of the more obese specimens of our own
species have been known to weigh-in at well over
half a ton. I would guess that's just about the size of
a walrus...a young one, anyway. By that logic, then,
shouldn't we deduce that such...adipose persons are
roughly equal in intelligence to an adolescent
walrus?

ML *[laughing]*: I don't know.

FV: On the other hand, didn't one Nobel Prize
winner apparently have a brain half, or a third the
average human size - what would normally be
associated with profound retardation?

ML: Who was that?

FV: Wasn't it Bergson? No...Anatole France, I think... Did I already mention this?

ML: I don't think so.

FV: I thought we were talking about France before... He was a member of the *Académie française* - we talked about that, right? Also the inspiration for Proust's Bergotte...allegedly.

ML: Is that right?

FV: Anyways, it was only the Literature prize...not one of the "difficult" ones. The issue, I think, is more that a walrus...or a whale, is not so equally equipped elsewhere. It hasn't the means to manipulate things as we do...to *express* whatever it may know... And, of course, it's somewhat romantic to consider how the planet's greatest geniuses may be tragically trapped in those cumbersome bodies...unable to fully manifest their genius. But, could it actually be, if they really are so smart, that they've simply abandoned any means of expression, evolved past the point of communication or creation, and retreated to the silence of the ocean...content just with knowing, whatever they know? Whales were, after all, once a bear-like creature...weren't they? Not as dexterous as us, I'm sure, but certainly more *expressive* than a whale.

ML: I suppose... But then, there are "whale songs," aren't there? And those dolphin chirps and clicks. They still seem to be expressing something.

FV: Ah, that's right. They may not be so smart after all. What about elephants, then? They seem fairly quiet.

ML: You've never heard an elephant before?

FV: Yes, but when they make a noise it's usually more of...an outburst, I think. An involuntary interjection, at best. More exclamational than linguistic, or...artistic, wouldn't you say?

ML: Pachyderm vocalisations aren't really my forté.

FV *[laughing]*: No...nor mine... This sort of reminds me of that old parable about the blind men trying to describe an elephant - each of them feeling a separate part —

ML: I think you already mentioned that one, didn't you?

FV: Did I?

ML: When you were talking about...what was it? Blind writers and braille...something about "the *gist* of life" —

FV: And our limitations...right. Now, see, if I *was* an elephant I wouldn't have forgotten that... But, of course, even elephants have their limits, too. Everything does...well...except, perhaps, *everything*. And if the universe...if reality is limitless, and everything that can be known about it, how smart could anything ever be? Big brain, small brain...no brain whatsoever - all of the knowledge that anything could know, when compared to the infinity of knowable things, must always equate to essentially nothing...mustn't it? Any life-form, then, would be alike in its ignorance; elephant, human, or sperm... Maybe that's the more fitting definition for 'life': *a completely ignorant thing.*

ML: Well, you would then have to include rocks, and water, and...everything else, wouldn't you?

FV: Yes... Perhaps 'ignorance' is not quite the right word, or...condition. What would it be? Perhaps... *'uncertainty'* is better suited. After all, it's one thing to just sit oblivious to the world, quite another to move against it. Surely it's a special type of ignorance which animates - one tinged with some unfounded hope...or anxiety. What else compels the plant's roots downward, or its branches up, but the *possibility* of nourishment - whether its out there or not? What propels the sperm forward but the *chance* of an egg? What drives the bacterium, or virus, from one host to another? What keeps the man going another day? Is it not the indeterminable contingency of something better...something more? Or, at least, the potential evasion of something less ...something worse?

ML: Of death?

FV: That ultimate limitation of life...that ultimate anxiety. The other common link, besides our uncertainty...that ultimate uncertainty...that most certain uncertainty. Perhaps *that*, then, is the best definition for 'life': *an almost completely uncertain thing; certain only of death.*

ML: I think I've read, though, there are certain

trees...and other organisms, that are thought to be practically immortal...at least, in theory.

FV: Immortal, or invincible?

ML: Well, not invincible.

FV: So they still could be killed.

ML: I suppose.

FV: Yet another uncertainty to live with, then. But at least a tree, presumably, is not conscious of its mortality...or its uncertainty. Still...one can't really be certain of that, either. Perhaps, just like us, it also grapples with both... Perhaps no life just gets on with the business of *living*, as from uncertainty can come anything...can come "what if?" And...*what if* it isn't all infinite? What if there is a limit, a goal...some *certainty* to be had? What if it can all be grasped, even by a tree...even by us...but then, just before reaching it, we're always struck down? On the cusp of satisfying one end, only to be foiled by the other... Or maybe we do reach it, then die... Then what?

ML: But "what if," somehow, you *can* live forever...immortal and invincible?

FV: Well, the problem with living forever, of course, is you have to live forever before you know you can do it. Even the gods, in this way, must always remain uncertain. Time trumps immortality...as uncertainty trumps "omniscience," for a knower can only ever know what it knows...never what it doesn't.

ML: Still, you wouldn't rather live forever anyways? Or, at least...in perpetuity? Just embrace the uncertainty, and leave it at that? Think of all the horrible drinks you could try!

FV *[laughing]*: You're not enjoying that? This is one of my favourites...

It's an odd thing transcribing a conversation which you have no recollection of. Bits and pieces start coming back, suggesting themselves - fragments which may, or may not have occurred, as if out of a dream. In this extended pause I can see Vanderson finishing his drink, then placing it down...he clasps a hand over the top of the glass, drawing up beads of condensation on his fingertips, then faintly dabbing his brow. He seems tired now, as if wearied by the weight of all the night's verbiage, the relentless onslaught of conflicting thoughts and intertwining ideas...then the drinks, of course. I have no memory of my own state at this time. I can only assume it was equally loaded.

As the topic of drinking still barely lingers, I at last break the silence by mentioning that curious bottle I had seen before. Strangely enough, Vanderson - this bar's regular of regulars, alchemist in residence - claims to have never noticed it. A brief discussion takes place as to what it could be, before deciding there was only one way to find out. "Two glasses of whatever that is," was our order. We'd have it straight this time, to see if we could guess what it was. As we wait for the mystery to arrive, Vanderson resumes the prior topic without missing a beat...

FV: No...I don't think I would want to go on forever.

Not as me, anyhow... Not as any living thing. Regardless if the universe is infinite or not, a life-form is finite...in senses and in thought; only so many receptors and nerve endings...only so many brain cells and synapses to process it all. Given an eternity to endure every possible combination of touch, taste, sight, and sound, the experience must inevitably begin to repeat itself...and repeat itself endlessly. Perception, in this way, truly *is* reality... and reality, then, truly is finite. Astronomically finite, granted, but finite nonetheless... Of course, one's finite memory then becomes a blessing, lest you live in some insufferable state of continuous *deja vu*. To live forever, it would seem, would be only to live witlessly unaware of the...perpetual purgatory that your actual existence truly is. But then...who's to say that's not what we're doing right now? Can you remember a time when you weren't alive? Personally, I can't remember much more before...well, I suppose, when I looked in that faucet.

ML: I can't remember much past two drinks ago.

FV: Only not living, it seems, erases the doubt. One must die, or never be born, if only to fully forget.

ML: Well, I know there's things in my life I wouldn't mind experiencing again...things I'd like to see, or do, countless more times...whether I remembered them or not.

FV: And many other things that you wouldn't, I'm sure.

ML: You take the good with the bad.

FV: You'd take them both, forever? The *infinitely* bad?

ML: And the infinitely *good*... Forever is a long time, anything could happen. All that uncertainty, as you say...things could get good and stay good.

FV: Or get bad, and get worse.

ML: Yes...or perhaps it's just a wash.

FV: I'd frankly rather things just stay bad.

ML: Jeez, you really are a pessimist!

FV *[laughing]*: Oh, I don't know... There's actually a sort of comfort in the belief that things can only get worse. It gives one an appreciation for the here-and-now...knowing that each and every moment may be as good as its ever going to get. And of course, in the end, if you do die... Well, I can't imagine living too happy a life...so much to lose. It only figures that the more miserable your life is the easier it is to lose it...and, if you can lose it all at any time, then any time spent un-enjoyed seems likely to be time well spent.

ML: That seems like a horrible way to live.

FV: Well, it's the best way I know...when living itself seems like a horrible way to live...to exist. When this..."active principle of existence" seems...in *principle*, its lowest principle...the lowest configuration of this *principal* principle... And even then, what of *it*? What of *existence*, then? Where does it get off imposing itself on everything...on nothing? Is it not simply the lowest...*thing*?

ML: So you're not a pessimist, then...merely a nihilist?

FV: But, I mean, what good has ever come from it, this...abomination? *Life*? *Thinking*? *Expression*? *Art*? This language which doesn't say anything? These definitions which have no meaning? All these lies? Tell me...why is it always that the more important a concept is, the more immediate that it seems - 'truth', 'life', 'existence' - the more unclear, the more... evasive its definition?

ML: What was 'existence', again?

FV: Did I read that one...? 'Exist'..."to be, have being, live."

ML: Alright... And what was 'be'?

FV: And 'be'...to '*be*'... "Live; exist..."

ML: Hmm...

FV: Also, "to have a state or quality." So then, '*quality*'..."attribute, characteristic, property." And '*attribute*'..."quality, property or characteristic of anything." Alright, '*anything*'...'anus', 'anvil', 'anxious', '*any*'..."one indefinitely." One *indefinitely*... 'Indefinite', 'indefinite'...so what is *that*? 'Indefeasible', 'indefensible'...'indelible'...where is it? It's not here? It's not even here!

ML: Looks like we've reached the end of the line.

FV: Yes...looks like... And perhaps we did... Perhaps that's it!

ML: What is?

FV: The out! The key! The beginning...and the end... Don't most scientists now predict some "end of the line" - an end to it all? Not just the death of things, but the...*annihilation* of *everything*? Some great contraction, or collapse...or some vast dissipation into eternal emptiness. Maybe it's all swallowed up by an immense black hole, which then swallows itself, but whatever the case this extinction is inevitable and absolute...so complete as to erase any and all evidence that this reality - this *existence* - ever took place... So complete that, perhaps, for all intents and purposes, it never really did!

ML: Come again?

FV: Don't you see? If this fate is truly...a *fait accompli* - if this "existence" is merely a *waiting*... then, what are we waiting for? Who's to say that any of this exists right now...or ever did, or ever will? And, if I'm not making any sense, wouldn't that only serve to bolster my point? In this...eschatology of science all the problems and contradictions of existence are cleanly swept away by the fact that all of...*this* simply never was! The universe, its events - its past, present, and future - all fictions! This experience, this presence, this very conversation never happened at all...and, of course, by the same token, neither did we!

ML: I think you've gone a step too far this time!

FV: I merely follow in the steps of my mentor: "Man creates what he calls history to conceal the apocalypse from himself..." Frye spoke there of biblical revelation. But I speak of...*God-knows-what*... We all do, perhaps... Our words that all point away from themselves...point away from a secret we seem to be hiding... Only from existence can come history - but from 'history' comes a 'story'...and any good story, as we know, is always better than the truth. Elaboration, embellishment, exaggeration... *something* instead of *nothing*... Did we not then, in fact, create —

And here the recorder cuts out on this fascinating, if somewhat strange (and somewhat lengthy) discussion. *[note: split into parts?]* I thank Gerry Vanderson most sincerely for agreeing to what must surely have seemed my equally strange request for this interview, and for sharing his time and thoughts. That he may not exactly be the most "important" or "influential literary figure of the day" - or that our conversation tended to veer slightly away from the topic of literature altogether - should not, I hope, count against either of us. In the spirit of Gerry's uncertainty (if not his discontent), I would like to think this interview could spell the start of better things ahead for everyone involved. After all, anything can happen...

As to the rest of what we discussed, I'll admit I'm still digesting most of it myself. I haven't any real summation, or final thoughts. This hangover, now three days on, is preventing me from forming many thoughts at all. When one is lost, however, it's often best to head back towards your starting point. So, in closing, rather than end on Vanderson's somewhat ominous aposiopesis, I thought I should bring everything around to translation again, and leave you, the reader, with one last quote...only this time in German.

I initially felt something French would be more appropriate, with regards to the main language of Vanderson's trade. Something from Daumal's *Night Of Serious Drinking* seemed fitting, but, after a brief skim, I couldn't find anything that fit all that well. Proust also crossed my mind, but...were to begin? I did find one passage from Drieu la Rochelle's *Le Feu Follet* that covered quite a lot of what *we* had covered. In the end, though, I felt it was a tad too long (if not a bit presumptuous, as well). So, finally, I settled on something a little shorter, perhaps a little more obvious...a little more honest. It's a fairly famous quote. Another old chestnut, maybe even a cliché. If I was to tell you it's from Wittgenstein you might be able to guess it without even needing a translation - but, still, it's the best way to end I can think of for now:

Wovon man nicht sprechen kann,
darüber muss man schweigen.

Taken with permission from: *Informem Quarterly - Vol. 1, Issue 4* (unpublished); Hour/Ohne Press (London, ON, 1999).

*There is a doctrine whispered in secret that man is a
prisoner who has no right to open the door and run away;
this is a great mystery which I do not quite understand.*
~ Plato attrib. Socrates, c. 360 BC
'Phaedo'

*Not nature, but the "genius of mankind,"
has knotted the hangman's noose
with which it can execute itself at any moment.*
~ C. G. Jung, 1952
'Answer to Job'

*No, slave, I will kill only thee
and let thee precede me!*
~ Anonymous, c. 1000 BC
'The Dialogue of Pessimism'

CITATIONS

CRIMINAL ACTS
Dan Garfat-Pratt

D. Garfat-Pratt
Professor M. Waugh
Bethridge College
HUMA104-01
November 29, 2006

I would like to start by saying that upon learning of this assignment to review a work of contemporary fiction I must admit to feeling more than a little dismayed. The time-honoured 'book report' is a chore I had rather hoped to be rid of by this stage in my education, and one I would frankly prefer to have never encountered in the first place.

Fiction in general holds little interest for me. Novels, in particular, arouse more suspicion than intrigue. It truly baffles me that any practitioner of make-believe should (especially in this day and age) feel the need to produce anything so gratuitous. The fact that certain examples of this fare can approach the length of your average dictionary seems inherently absurd - nearly as absurd as the desire to read such a thing. To be honest, I've simply never felt the need to escape the affairs of my own life for any such period of time required to engage these ponderous tales.

Nevertheless, year after year, like a classroom Sisyphus, I am forced to indulge the weight of some obese tome, to extract a message or moral from the wadding of its tedious descriptions, regurgitate my inevitably insightless disinterest in the form of a paper such as this, and then inflict that drivel back onto you, the teacher, thus completing some ridiculous circuit of pointless exasperation.

At this juncture you may wonder, then, why I chose English as an elective in this, my final semester of college. In hindsight I might well ask myself the same question. Having little, if any, interest in the alternatives provided, though, and having a modicum of previous success in the subject, it would seem my decision was simply a matter of picking the least of multiple evils. Of course, I don't mean to paint this particular class or subject as being literally 'evil' in any way, but I was hoping for more of a technical/practical approach to the subject this time around, as opposed to the usual focus on its 'creative' aspects.

All this being said, it may surprise you to learn that I do consider myself *reasonably* well-read (if not by choice). Hounded as I have been throughout my schooling by such tasks as this, I've had imposed on me the opportunity to ingest a great diversity of various writings. And I won't deny that I have, *on occasion*, been impressed by certain works of *past* invention. I do, however, think the entire industry would have done well to conclude around the time of Solomon's "Nothing new under the sun" treatise. It is, you see, the 'contemporary' facet of this assignment which most troubles me.

I have come to suspect that literature (along with most every other artistic form) has long since starved from a lack of ideas; the stench of its corpse barley hidden now by a thin application of stylistic masking agents which fool only the most foolish among us. I realize this is, of course, the typically 'post-modern' observation/complaint, yet as objectionable as I find such a categorization, I find it even harder to argue against the notion that we have now arrived at the point where human imagination has simply collapsed in on itself, leaving everyone with only its wreckage to rebuild. You must, therefore, understand my confusion in regards to what I might possibly hope to say, with any originality, about that which offers so little (if anything) original to say itself.

In short, I find reading to be only time consuming; writing about it even more so. Nevertheless, I still welcome the chance to be corrected and enlightened (I don't honestly hope to argue my way out of this assignment anyway). But, I would like to think that my concerns may allow grounds for a certain degree of compromise. Thus, in the faint hope of circumventing at least some of this assignment's inherent aggravation, I have chosen to examine not a book, but an album, where conceit to trends and repetition falls generally within the domain of the music, while the words - the ideas - however unrefined, might (at least, theoretically) remain truer to some sort of 'spirit', for lack of a better word.

The album which I propose to examine is *Don Jail Roadway* - the most recent offering of a rather unknown local act called Chapeau. The primary lyricist of this outfit is apparently one E. Tancarville, though little else is know to me of either him or his band. I should state that I am not terribly familiar with Chapeau's previous output. In point of fact I don't much care for their music and would not wish to probe it any further than I already have. The lyrics of this particular release, on the other hand, struck me as sufficiently interesting to warrant further criticism (at least, as long as I'm obligated to criticise). I will therefore separate Mr. Tancarville and his lyrical contributions from Chapeau the musical entity, leaving analysis of the latter to those more inclined.

DJR (as I will abbreviate the album from hereon out) takes the form of what is known as a 'concept album'. Such works, as you may know, are distinguished from ordinary albums in that all of the songs revolve around a common theme, often telling a story (as *DJR* does), with the tracks acting like chapters, or acts in a play. At only 30 minutes in length *DJR* is rather short by the standards of most concept albums (and by most albums in general) - but by no means is this album short on concepts (obscure as some of them may be). Its entire package is a bit of a puzzle: artwork replete with cryptic reference and symbolism; song titles which, at first glance, don't seem to have any relation to their content; and then, of course, there are the songs themselves, which I will now précis in sequence:

***

The Don Jail, as you probably know, is that infamous correctional facility overlooking the Don river valley near the intersection of Gerrard and Broadview. Upon consultation with any Toronto street map you will also find that there is, in fact, a Don Jail Roadway leading into the prison. This reference is but the first in a long line of not exactly subtle metaphors.

As we will see, the scope of the album concerns not only crime, but a central figure mired in a state of inescapable uncertainty - the proverbial 'prisoner of doubt'. *DJR*'s opening refrain, "It's Hard Not to

Die", makes clear this conception straight from the outset. Taking the form of a brief soliloquy, confided by the aforementioned protagonist, the whole of the lyrics read as follows:

If I only knew what I wanted surely I could steal it.
There's got to be something that I need to get along.
If I had to take a life tonight God knows I would take it.
I'd break any law you could find, commit any crime
(wouldn't I?).

In a commendable act of foreshadowing these four lines manage to establish all of the album's major themes: crime, religion, death and uncertainty; tying them all together while hinting at their eventual resolution within the work. Yet, at this initial juncture, there's actually little else to be said as its significance (as will soon become obvious) tends to unfold during the subsequent pieces - which, from here on in, I will flesh out in further detail.

The second song, "Deathgrip on Living", begins with a well known passage from Chapter 11 of the Book of Genesis:

And they said: Go to, let us build us a city and a tower,
whose top may reach unto heaven; And let us make us a
name, lest we be scattered abroad upon the face of the
whole earth.

While serving as a thinly veiled allusion to the story's setting (certainly not the first time that the 'CN Tower / Tower of Babel' correlation has been made), the quotation also addresses this particular song's subject matter: identity. The song not only introduces us to our protagonist's identity, but establishes the very concept of 'making a name' for one's self as a function of crucial importance - one must latch onto an identity, as the above line is interpreted, lest one be scattered philosophically.

In "Deathgrip" we learn our hero has made a name for himself as a criminal subsisting on the societal fringe. He assumes the role of a murderous thug - "*a dead-eyed, gun-slinging killer*" - known throughout the city for his brutal deeds. But this identity is later revealed to be only a front, as he confesses: "*I'm really just a conman (but conning who?)*" His rough-hewn exterior is only an armour against the harsh and fearful circumstances he finds himself in (both environmental and internal). What we assume to have in the 'conman' character is a clear archetype of existential dread. Not only must he endure the daily turmoil which accompanies a criminal lifestyle, but his mind is constantly racked by deeper questions of meaning, doubt, and of course, identity - questions put even further into focus when he is confronted by the story's next character, a local crime boss.

This "*north end chief*", as he's described, has presumably been taken in by rumours of the conman's fabricated exploits, and wills to procure his services, saying: "*I need three bodies, and I don't mean maybe.*" The conman attempts to talk his way out of the situation, but to no avail, conceding to himself: "*It seems my bad reputation's put me in a worse position.*" Although the identities of the proposed victims are not disclosed it is apparent that the act of killing itself, despite being the very act he has based his "*bad reputation*" on, is now the main source of the conman's growing consternation:

They say the code of the con is to know just enough about everything so you can lie about anything,
But I wouldn't know murder if it crept up slowly, put a hand on my mouth and stuck a knife right through me.

He is painted into a corner at this point. His only solace is the boss' promise of $100,000 should he somehow manage to fulfill his end of the contract. But it's an incentive which lends only to tie further knots into his escalating identity crisis. "*For that kind of bread...*" the conman ponders, "*who am I to say who I am?*"

The song then ends as it began, departing on biblical verse (Isaiah 1:21):

> *How is the faithful city become an harlot!*
> *It was full of judgment; righteousness lodged in it;*
> *But now murderers.*

Through this quotation the conman's intentions seem to be clear, even if his resolve has yet to firm. We can also assume this to be a comment on the city's gradual shift away from its famous, if never entirely accurate 'Toronto the Good' persona.

In act 3, "From Life & Death to Living Dead" we meet the album's third character. The conman has gone to seek guidance and, in fact, support from an unnamed "doctor" (one assumes to be a psychiatrist of sorts) so as to carry out the villainous deed. The doctor, however, is none too keen, saying: "*It's not my place to counsel crime. I don't intend to waste our time.*" But the conman persists and proceeds to list off a series of justifications in his own support. First he reasons that the targets are simply worthless criminals: "*A clutch of hoods, of thieves like me.*" He then appends this reasoning to a biological argument, placing himself (and presumably the rest of humanity) within the rogue's gallery of creation, citing the likes of "*killer whales, vampire bats, strangler figs,*" and (bizarrely) "*pedophile mushrooms*". In a concession to the ruthless law of nature, that one can only live by exploiting the lives of others, he follows by saying: "*I wouldn't touch the innocent, whoever they are.*"

He then pronounces: "*We take lesser lives just by waking up. So what am I scared of?*", deferring to the argument that we are all mass murderers at one scale or another, unwittingly killing countless microbial beings during the course of our daily routine (not to mention all of the higher life-forms which we consciously deem to be either food or disposable vermin). And if we take some forms of life so easily, the conman reckons, what difference is there in taking another? But clearly it isn't as easy for him as his logic supposes it should be.

At this point the doctor draws a clear distinction: "*To harm your own, to kill your kind, you'd only kill yourself you'll find,*" to which our budding assassin replies: "*But if I'm willing to kill maybe I deserve to die,*" and again: "*...so who am I scared of?*" It's a curious bit of self-fulfilling reasoning. Here he also interjects the possibility of some external source of judgment by which the thinking grows even more entangled:

> *Everyone gets what they deserve,*
> *But what's 'deserve'? - a man-made term.*
> *Let me ask you, is there anything more preposterous*
> *Than two agreeing, nodding heads?*
> *Is the Bible true because it says it is?*

His worries have turned from a personal dilemma to a problem of more universal concern. He has come to recognize an alarming lack of reference in his thought. We are, he now fears to think, alone in the pursuit of knowledge and consensus. "Sole judge of truth, in endless error hurl'd", as Pope described this condition. It's a situation which, to some, necessitates the supernatural, and the conman now pursues this route - albeit, with equal reservation.

The piece ends with the desperate plea: "*Doctor, please encourage me*", which trails off into silence without an answer. Having lost faith in human reinforcement the conman will now seek guidance in the sacrosanct. One gets the sense that his deadly mission is one of the few things he has left to cling to now, and he'll go to any length in order to find some meaning in it - abiding by the doctrine that one must believe in something, even if one doesn't truly believe it.

In the fourth chapter, entitled "Death by Death Defiance", we are confronted with what appears to be a fourth, female character. Referred to as a "*rock hardened criminal*", she appears inexplicably as some strange misleader and mistreater of those she seduces. But it is likely the listener/reader who is somewhat misled. I suspect this moniker refers not so much to the callous demeanor of a new character, but to the song itself - music and lyrics both awash in the stylistic clichés of the 'rock' genre. As it turns out, this diversion is only a brief prelude to what reveals itself as yet another inner dialogue in which the conman now seeks a biblical proxy for the encouragement his doctor either could not, or would not give.

As the music changes so changes the direction of his discourse. Now our protagonist addresses a whole internal audience: "*Can I lend word to the transgressors here among us?*" He then proceeds to cite "*one little bad verse from this good book*" - namely Galatians 5:4:

> *Christ is become of no effect unto you,*
> *whosoever of you are justified by the law;*

ye are fallen from grace.

It should be noted that this passage is part of sermon given by Paul against the custom of circumcision. It seems a curious reference at first, but when viewed in isolation it takes on a host of ulterior implications. This selective act itself may be remarking on an all too common practice among the faithful of hand-picking such lines to be used completely out of context in order to justify any number of dubious ends. But, as we've already seen, Tancarville tends to view the testaments with a more interpretive eye, encouraging us to read between the lines.

This one particular law may be extended outward to encompass all laws, even the very concept of law. Paul himself claims in a previous verse that once a man resigns to the adherence of one law he becomes "a debtor to the whole of the law", caught in the obsessive dogmatism of taboo and ritual; worshiping at the alter of yet another false idol. But Tancarville and his conman take this notion further still, applying it to the final, inescapable law which governs our very thoughts: logic.

In concordance with a long pessimistic tradition (Schopenhauer, Unamuno, Cioran) the conman now delves into Paradise Lost territory: chapter 3 of Genesis and history's first recorded crime. The aforementioned "*rock hardened criminal*", it must now be assumed, is an allusion to Eve, while the conman embodies the role of both Adam and the serpent, willfully facilitating his own temptation. He reads humanity's banishment from the garden not as a reprimand meted out by some vindictive, insecure God; nor does he consider the tree of knowledge an arbitrary prop in some petty test of obedience. God's edict was a warning, a sincere word of caution. It is the act of eating the fruit which was itself the punishment. "*You're gonna get sick eating that fruit...*" the conman warns himself, "*You're gonna get too damned smart for your own damn good.*" But of course, the fruit has long already been consumed.

To the conman Eden was not a physical place, but a primordial state of mind - blissful and sate, untroubled by the treacherous lure of understanding. But it's a state now forever inaccessible. Once the fruit of knowledge has been consumed we're set off on a journey of no return. Down that proverbial slippery slope (that *Don Jail Roadway*), from reason to truth and ultimately to meaning - a vague, troublesome concept separated from experience by an infinite regress of questioning. Endless inquiry towards an endlessly receding aim; answers each as unfulfilling as the last, or the next. Despite the fig leaf artifice of our intellect, the conman "*still feels naked the way we are*", conceding: "*The law of answers only justifies more questions.*" To him, the illusion of progress is sentience's fall from grace. It is, as Dostoevsky's *Underground Man* observes, so that "an intelligent man cannot seriously become anything"...save only, perhaps, a mere philosopher.

It's a mordant line of reasoning which leads inexorably to reason itself, and it is here where the conman trespasses that bizarre threshold from the paralyzing effects of mere uncertainty to a kind of transcendent meta-doubt:

> *And the last question you can ask is*
> *'do you really know what you know?'*
> *But there ain't no way of knowing*
> *'cause my hallowed knowledge tells me so.*

He has run astern of the paradox at the very heart of

thought; the basic introduction to any study of epistemology: how is one to determine the validity of logic without using logic in one's determination? It's from this dizzying vantage that one begins to glimpse the faintly perceptible workings of the mind's own formal system, as susceptible to Gödel's insidious theorem as any other; "*completely limited by unlimited incompleteness*".

The conman realizes that, in the end, logic is as much a matter of faith as the word of God, or anything else - a point that even the most ardent logician must grudgingly concede. Such is the nature of thought that we can never really *know* anything. We can only *think* we *know* (semantics aside). As Borges was led to ponder of our intellect: "Is this a legitimate instrument of investigation or only a bad habit?" It's a vexing question which, much to the chagrin of our conman, is essentially unanswerable. Still, despite it's imposition, most are duly content to abide by the law of logic as little immediate ill ever seems to come of it. Rather, it's usually seen as beneficial in alleviating the host of other burdens imposed by life. But the conman remains the skeptic and bends this infliction to his own device:

My head is a prison I've been locked in from the start,
So if I'm treated like a criminal I might as well play the
part.

This seems a rather trite motto to endorse, similar to what one might expect of your typical adolescent malcontent. Yet it forms in our hero the groundswell of an unstoppable tide, a wholesale transition from Underground Man to Raskolnikov, culminating in a resound equal parts resignation and affirmation: "*I am a criminal!*" It is a resound born not of any desperate social or economic conditions, nor of any baser urge towards simple rebellion or malevolence.

Here is the philosophical offender, at once totally free and determinist - the logical outcome of the failure of logic.

Part 5, "L'Amour de Mort" is a rather strange departure - in more ways than one. As the title would suggest the lyrics of this song are entirely in French, and despite Mr. Tancarville's apparent (or, at least, assumed) French ancestry, it is obvious that French is not his native tongue. The lyrics range from grammatically crude to downright bewildering. And the choice of language seems all the more puzzling when considering the subject matter of the song relates to ancient Mesoamerica. Whatever the reason for this strange combination, the result is a bit of a muddle. However, if one takes the time to decipher its libretto (which, admittedly, I'm only partially convinced I have done), one discovers a narrative almost as interesting as Tancarville's (mis)use of the Gallic vocabulary.

The conman sings in praise of the people who built the great temple complex Teotihuacán, a culture which he describes as continually "*at war with peace, and at peace with war*". Their enemy: the gods themselves. They claim descendance from the Promethean feathered serpent Quetzalcoatl, whom it is said stole from the gods the very seed of life. And it is this possibility - that our life, as stolen property, was never meant to be ours - which leads the conman to postulate: "*Perhaps this is why life does not quite make sense.*" The correlation here between this creation myth and that of Original Sin is striking: two accounts of human conception born of a primal crime, perpetrated at the behest of a mysterious snake.

The conman takes encouragement in the audacity of this culture, willing to defy even the divine. He refers to the later Aztecs' pleasure in eventually fighting "*a battle they were destined to lose*" against Quetzalcoatl himself, famously misperceived in the form of an invading Hernán Cortés. At the same time he sees in his own impending act of defiance a sense of unavoidable duty, likened to the grim act of compensation these early Mexicans would regularly make in atonement for the crime of their heavenly idol:

> *Fighting against time, when the gods would inevitably reclaim what was theirs, this clever race knew how to delay them; to prolong what little time they had left: A human sacrifice, every now and then, until there was nobody left to kill.*

Like grains of sand in a great apocalyptic hour glass, each immolation engorges the pile of gruesome tribute while counting down the moments towards an imminent doom. This unsettling image makes clear the conman's intent. He has engaged in a mission of total annihilation, prepared to pay in full what he calls "*the price for life*".

For the final act, "Waiting to Die (And the Suspense is Killing Me)", Tancarville reverts (thankfully) to English, and the conman is once again in conference with the doctor. But the doctor has suddenly taken a much more proactive interest in the conman's scheme, informing him: "*We both know you're incapable of doing this without me.*" He demands to know the identity of the three intended victims, and it is here where the thickening plot becomes at once transparent:

> *Did I say three? I suppose that's fitting.*
> *A holy ghost in our strange trinity,*

A Platonic third man in our 'felosophy'.

If it was not yet obvious, Tancarville now makes it perfectly blatant: the conman, the doctor, and the crime boss; Adam, Eve, and the serpent; ego, superego, and id - all a trinity of trinities comprising one singular self - instigator, perpetrator, and victim in one.

With one last gasp of pluralism the fading essence of our hero's doctor persona lifts a line directly from Jesus at the last supper: "*Behold, the hands of my betrayer are with me at the table.*" The crux of this self-crucifixion is lain bare, the conman has pulled-off his ultimate con. He has fulfilled the role of Judas to himself and will now die, Christ-like, for the sins of his mind.

As the panning voices in his head slowly merge into one, our protagonist spells out this final resolution:

> *There's only room for one criminal,*
> *Only time for one last crime,*
> *One plus two minus three: Felo de se.*

Crime against the self - the last offence of a perpetual offender, locked down in a world of unjust laws. The album ends with a reprise of all the various transgressions which amount to one intolerable circumstance. The prisoner of doubt ends his stint in the Don Jail, released to the custody of that final question mark which punctuates every life sentence.

***

Now then, what are we to extract from the dense convolution of metaphor and symbolism that is *Don*

Jail Roadway? Has Tancarville put forward anything of novel substance? Has he revived any notions which have since passed from the collective consciousness? To be sure, his reading of the Bible as an allegorical endorsement for crime, ignorance and suicide is, if nothing else, a peculiar interpretation. But the prevailing sentiment of this work is one as old as Ecclesiastes. Tancarville's 'mind as prison' analogy is certainly one of the most belaboured clichés in the canon, while his conman's anomic view of logic is, by this stage, little more than echo. That this view should compel the conman to take his own life does, however, raise a few additional questions.

We must ask: is the protagonist's role as a 'conman' indicative of a stance against suicide or rather a statement of necessity? Tancarville appears to have left *DJR* sufficiently vague as to allow for just such speculation, possibly employing the old tactic of leaving enough room for the critics to finish his masterpiece for him. Of course, it is more often the case that vagueness on the page (or disc) is simply the result of vagueness in the mind, and as Tancarville hasn't left quite enough room for a masterpiece, I am inclined to suspect this latter scenario. Unfortunately, such ambiguity does not make for compelling book report fodder (if such a thing exists). So, for the sake of nothing else than filling up pages, let us attempt to complete some of Mr. Tancarville's thoughts.

Looking anew at such song titles as "Deathgrip on Living" and "Death by Death Defiance", he seems to be expressing what can be seen as the almost morbid fascination we have with life. From here we are forced to reevaluate the conman character. Deceived as he might have been into suicide, Tancarville's hero was, as you'll remember, a conman from the beginning. It's an apt analogy to what could be perceived as the great confidence scheme we all perpetrate against each other, and ourselves; putting on the brave facades of wisdom and understanding, while swindling our souls into yet another day.

When considering the slope of dilemmas which hastened the conman's descent, one may be reminded of a riddle first encountered by most in their childhood (and usually dismissed or forgotten around the same time) - that being: assuming that the 'insane' will often figure themselves to be 'sane', how does one truthfully discern which group they belong to?

On the rare occasions when this problem is taken seriously and duly contemplated people generally come to one of two conclusions - the first being that the very concept of sanity is tenuous at best. Indeed, over the years some of the 'sanest' minds have seemed at a loss to find any sense of the rational in this world. One might recall Twain's despondent observation that "Nature itself is insane." On the other hand, at a certain, inexplicable level, it can seem that it does not even make sense that the world, itself, should 'make sense'.

The second conclusion usually drawn is that, as long one gets out of life what they want, the matter of mental wellness is essentially moot. But then, what is it exactly that either the sane or insane person should want? If one determines his own needs and desires, should an insane mind be trusted with such a decision? What if all that one wants is to know if he is sane? Surely, at the most basic level, one is compelled by the pleasure principle. One simply wants happiness; satisfaction, fulfilment, contentment - call it what you will - this is the fuel which life runs on. The having of it sustains life and the pursuit of it propels life. But you should note a slight circularity here, in that we seek from life the very thing which perpetuates it. We are, for whatever reason, and for whatever it's worth, compelled to be alive.

Now, to most, this seems a rather harmless loop. And it's little wonder that anyone complicit with this circumstance would uphold their life (and the lives of anyone else which compliment their own) to the furthest ends. Suicide is an unthinkable notion for those who find happiness in simply finding happiness (or those who, at least, hold out hope that one day they will). But what concern is it of these life-affirmers if some should act from an opposing view? Here is perhaps the one point of contention that *DJR* suitably invokes.

It does give one pause to think that the act of suicide is so proscribed as to have once been (and in many places still is) considered criminal (i.e.: *felo de se*). Even among the more liberal societies, suicide is still tacitly portrayed as a cowardly act - 'the easy way out' as it's commonly termed - dismissed in almost smug, self-congratulatory tones as merely a desperate play by incompetent players in some trivial game. A game in which they, themselves, are apparent authorities. Needless to say, this is usually just an obvious attempt to mask and suppress their own fear and insecurity when confronting the subject. The truth, of course, is that when committed with full faculty, suicide is likely the most difficult, indeed the most 'courageous' act that anyone can perform.

Despite constant propaganda to the contrary, it is life which is the 'easier' of the two to maintain. Mind and body alike prove time and again that they are capable of enduring untold sufferings and indignities so as to extend their selfish persistence. I would, in fact, wager that throughout the course of history all the heroic accounts of 'survival against the odds' far outweigh the cases of *true* suicide. Rare is the being which, while fully sound of mind (relatively speaking, of course), combats the unconscious forces willing its own perpetuation. It is, in fact, unheard of (at least to me) for any organism other than the human to commit this act on any notable scale - perhaps evidence of our advanced(?) evolution.

Suicide's craven reputation certainly isn't helped by the seemingly petty crises which often precipitate it. But, in an atmosphere of absurdity and relativism, pettiness is well spread amongst all things. I would think, instead, that the simple, innate urge to self-preservation is more catalytic to this adverse view. The suicide of one can raise troubling, potentially deadly doubts among others, so the social body acts to fight this contagion; mobilized in a subconscious call to arms. Even those who probe life to it's most dispassionate ends often seem compelled to perpetuate the notion of suicide as some great taboo, in spite of a host of presumptions which would tend to excuse, if not support it.

Take the biologist, for example, who views himself and his evolution as nothing but an ancient series of mutations and accidents, his life and his mind just some exploited mistake; the intelligent vehicle of mindless propagation. His brain is nothing but a complex of filters and gates, there only to protect his genetic seed. His consciousness, merely another accidental by-product. If this is so, then who are we to dispute our DNA's agenda? If survival (to whatever end) of the 'fittest' genes is paramount, then surely those 'unfit' should not survive; and one would assume any mechanism prone to self-destruction would be, at core, defective in the first place.

Then there is the cosmologist, who views himself as nothing but a manipulation of atoms; his mind configured out of randomness into the tool a vast, blind universe might use to perceive itself. If this is so then truly "all is vanity". What could be more pleasing to the cosmic narcissist than to gaze eternally with a billion eyes into the mirror that is himself? What fault, however, if certain eyes ultimately don't like what they see?

Of course, there is the spiritual one who invariably views himself as some corrupted soul estranged from some perfect purity - made so, apparently, through some strange lapse of perfection. If this is so, then we are certainly provided a lifetime of questions, such as: how can perfection ever be recognized, let alone attained, by the intrinsically imperfect? How sacred is any purity which allows corruption in the first place? And, once born into this, what state is more perfect or pure than death?

And then there is the philosopher, with no firm view at all. Content only to claim deeper insight than the next; fit only to destroy the illusions of all possible worlds, then pose stoically atop their ruins, waiting then to be trodden himself by those seeking even broader perspectives. So it is that, just as nature abhors a vacuum, philosophy abhors an answer, for once the truth is truly attained, the game is truly up. So the philosopher goes on, as do all the rest, flying in the face of their own aimless futility. It seems they couldn't stop themselves even if they wanted to. Whether fueled by some uncontrollable hope that there's still something unknown to be gained from persisting, or whether retreating in disgrace behind a dense smog of dissonance, still they go on - and all the while preaching blind, empty devotions to relative 'complexity' or the ambiguous 'wonder of it all'.

There's no end to the diversions we employ. But one makes his own meanings as the counterfeiter prints his own money: both know full well that the value of either rests solely in the gullibility of its recipient. Such forgery is then rendered doubly absurd if one takes, with Schopenhauer, the stance that life at any rate is "a business that does not cover its costs." Yet most still manage to eke out a living borrowing against that which carries little, if any currency. Camus' Sisyphus is even happy to subsist on a steady diet of enlightened disdain for his own ridiculous plight. But for Tancarville's conman even this cannot offer succor. He must reject any scornful apprehension of the long pointless struggle. His suspicion of reason renders any analysis of 'absurdity' absurd in its own right (a glitch the absurdist would no doubt embrace).

To subscribe and adhere to any life philosophy is to commit to at least some belief - whether that be to a god, or to science, or perhaps something less presumptuous such as the Cartesian 'doubt away everything and there will still remain doubt'. In any event, one must assume at least some faint grasp of the reality of either the world or the self before formulating a plan of action to which it accords. Yet this is a leap the conman is presumably incapable of. From his standpoint one does not understand his own limitations, he simply functions according to them.

The conman has pushed his mind to a threadbare extreme, and "he that diggeth a pit shall fall into it." He is gripped by that strangely convincing deduction that the very act of deduction itself is strangely unconvincing. Logic seems purpose-built and hopelessly destined to strive toward self-made concepts it can never fully attain, and while it circuitously insists on its own validity, it warns that one who dines at such round tables can never expect to leave with their appetite satisfied.

Arriving at this impasse one might attempt to persuade the conman into heeding intuition, or some other recondite process by which logic is deemed unnecessary. Yet the conman could only wonder if such processes are not simply ulterior forms of logic operating at a subconscious level (assuming one in his state could even experience or recognize these processes). It is, after all, a logical act of persuasion which would lead him to favour any such perceived alternative in the first place. Should one accept a method by means of another method which they would reject? Well, not logically. But then, to the conman, logic seems to do of itself just this!

Others, having traveled this far along reason's twisting path, may arrive back where they presumably started, taking their thoughts and experience at face value. They will see fit to build from 'truths' which they suppose to be 'inherent', pointing to consistent results in an external world as proof of logic's reliability, and inviting the conman to do the same. But, of course, the conman must first trust his logic that there is such a delineation of worlds to be made - or that anything he observes is to be believed in the first place. And even then, is equating a 'result' with a 'proof' not simply another untenable, logical function?

Now, to most, such unbridled skepticism may border on, if not inhabit, the ludicrous - a lot of needless worry based on useless, unprovable misgivings. But to the conman and his ilk, the burden of proof always falls with the faithful. Before making converts to the church of inference one must first disprove the distressing possibilities of solipsism or malevolent illusion, lest they too enter the realm of the ridiculous. A case for proof itself must even be made! I believe it was Gorgias who was first to posit the impossibility of ever prooving anything - in which case, it might as well have been me to first propose this idea, just now. And who's to say otherwise? Surely not our conman. Indeed, it's an isolated world in which he dwells, at complete loggerheads with those on the outside, never to be convinced of anything. Neither scrutiny, nor dismissal, nor shifting blame to the question can unravel this intrusive paradox. Even when facing a corner the shadow of doubt still looms large.

Where both conception and perception are called into doubt there is little room for certainty of any kind. As in the words of Blake, "he who doubts from what he sees will ne'er believe, do what you please." Here Blake echos the sentiments of Thomas Reid who famously conceded the futility of "beating" (by way of argument at least) the doubter of one's own faculties from the "stronghold" of his "metaphysically lunacy." He must instead "be left to enjoy his skepticism."

Still Reid, ever faithful to the indubitability of common sense, denies that the skeptic really takes his own reservations seriously on the grounds that to do so "does violence to our constitution." Self-evident truths persist in their veracity because belief in them aids in our own persistence. The self-professed doubter-of-all-things who holds a pistol to his head does not, in his heart of hearts, truly believe that anything but his own certain death would result from pulling the trigger, and so, in the end, he does not. But, putting meta-doubt in one's own doubt aside, what else should be expected from a being who has surely undergone a lifetime of indoctrination in such "common sense" prior to any sort of skeptical revelation; from just another member of a species seemingly prone to grand hypocrisies of these kinds in the first place? What if he honestly does not "enjoy his skepticism?" Did it not also rise from his own precious constitution? What evidence is there to support the value of its persistence? What evidence that it does not deserve violence?

Yet still, in the ubiquity of the conman's suspicions, the option of death seems equally arbitrary. There's no guarantee that it would improve his lot, or make *any* difference whatsoever. There's really no guarantee of an option at all. But, to turn a phrase of Camus back against him: "It is always easy to be logical. It is almost impossible to be logical to the bitter end." By his very descent towards an absolute uncertainty the conman is led to a curious reserve of optimism, realizing that while one may have to live with life, death - in all its majestic uncertainty - might yet, for all he knows, yield his salvation. Beneath the facade of knowledge and logical progress, it is actually our ignorance that truly propels us.

He has taken a stand (however useless it may be) against the perverse, tyrannical void of his experience; that dark ouroboros which ultimately offers no authentic happiness, only occasional and all too brief moments of distraction from the perpetual onslaught of itself. The conman has struck directly at the root of his dilemma, and in doing so evokes the names of other pathfinders who took similar, exceptional stands, and left in their wake generations of 'thinkers' - awash in their excuses and meaningless aporetics - scrambling to justify their own questionable continuation. "*Quid ad hominem claustra carcer custodia? Liberum ostium habet.*"

Or, to be a little less grand, it might be said the conman has, at least, rid the world of yet another redundant philosopher...except, of course, this was only a fiction. Whether *DJR* was a manifesto or merely a toothless 'thought experiment' we may never know - but considering the long tradition of pessimistic expression from which it draws, and the traditionally low rate of appropriate response to such outcries, I feel there is little risk of *DJR* inspiring any significant action in either its author or anyone else.

And so ends my interpretation of this album. Admittedly, I may have read too much into its lyrics. Then again, I may not have read enough. In truth I tire of reading now; of writing, even more so. I'm only relieved to consider, as I now embark on a new life away from the classroom, that this will surely be the last time that I'm ever required to write about reading.

In summary: for all its grand contrivance, *Don Jail*

Roadway ultimately says nothing more novel, insightful, or useful about our 'condition' than anything I myself have just said in reviewing it. But then, in this age where it's no longer about what you say, but how you say it, *DJR* might still reach a certain audience not yet acquainted with the thoughts it expounds. Perhaps even those pre-versed in such ideas may find occasion for a refresher of sorts. Caught as we are, in this vortex of life, I suppose we all oblige reminders of that which we already know; gladly forgetting, time and again, if only to keep the conversation going - not that anything fruitful ever seems to come of it. What might be gleaned if we ever truly took anything to heart? One can only wonder. As things stand, everything under the sun remains old, and it all may be useless in any case.

*

Dan,

Unfortunately I am unable to grade this paper. A review of a CD is simply not an appropriate substitute for a book report. The guidelines for this assignment were made quite clear, and I find it rather disappointing that you would so flagrantly disregard them.

As for the content of what you did submit, there are many inadequacies in both form and format (thesis statement, bibliography, word count, double spacing, etc.). I will also remind you that an academic essay of this sort is not a suitable platform from which to air personal grievances regarding the curriculum.

I would like you to submit another paper, on another <u>book</u>. If you are interested in philosophical topics there are many proper works of literature I could suggest.

Please see me after class,
Prof. Waugh

Taken with permission from: *Bethridge Student Archives*; Bethridge College of Applied Arts (Toronto, 2006).

CITATIONS

[Man] could no less adequately be defined as a laughing animal [...] And this is indeed something to marvel at: that man, who is the most afflicted and the most miserable of all creatures, should possess the faculty of laughter, which is alien to every other animal.
~ Giacomo Leopardi, 1824
'In Praise of Birds'

There is nothing but jest - or something intermediate to jest and tragedy; That ours is not an existence but an utterance.
~ Charles Fort, 1919
'The Book of the Damned'

Do not remain silent, master, do not remain silent! If you do not open your mouth, your opponent will have a free hand!
~ Anonymous, c. 1000 BC
'The Dialogue of Pessimism'

CITATIONS

OPEN MIC
J. Ross Clara

DRAMATIS PERSONAE:
A Host
A Comedian
A Heckler
A Chorus of audience members

SCENE:
The stage of a comedy club, May 1984. Proverbial brick wall backdrop. A single microphone stand placed in the centre. The Heckler and Chorus are voiced from offstage and remain unseen for the duration of the play.

*

The curtain raises on the Host - alone, centre stage, microphone in one hand, set list in the other. Dying laughter and applause are heard from the Chorus as the play begins...

HOST: OK, let's keep this going for our next comic! He only listed his name as "Alex," so Alex, if you're back there...

After a few uncertain moments the Comedian takes the stage.

HOST: Let's hear it for Alex!

The Chorus applauds and the Host hands over the microphone.

COMEDIAN (*to the Host*): That's not my name.

HOST: Sorry, did I read this wrong? It looks like "Alex"...

COMEDIAN: No, that's right.

HOST: You wrote in "Alex?"

COMEDIAN: Yes, but that's not my name.

The Chorus laughs.

HOST: Alright... Well, introduce yourself, then! The next five minutes is your's...

The Host leaves the stage. The Comedian places the microphone into the stand, then struggles to lower it into a suitable position.

COMEDIAN (*to himself, yet audible*): What kind of hymie fuckin' conspiracy is this?

Confused/hesitant laughter from the Chorus. After some prolonged fumbling the Comedian gives up his struggle and removes the microphone from the stand.

COMEDIAN: So, any of you ever have that dream where the triangular eyes turn into hexagons?

Silence.

COMEDIAN: No...? I had the strangest dream last night. I think I was in Hell, or something. It was kind of like one of those ball pits you see kids playing in, you know? I was sunk down in this pit, engulfed by balls... Balls all around me... My whole world was these balls, and I was just sinking down and down and down... Suffocating...

Silence.

COMEDIAN: I always thought Hell would be more like that show *Parlez-moi*. You remember that show? On TVO? With the clown that taught you French... Maybe not Hell. Just any sort of afterlife, I guess. I always pictured it that way... Some sparse, strange TV set with some fake, endless monochrome backdrop... And everyone there, if there's anyone there, just speaking some bewildering, nonsensical gibberish...

Faint, confused muttering from the Chorus.

COMEDIAN: Let's see, what else... Oh, speaking of TV and the afterlife, I see they're coming out with a movie based on the old *Ghost Busters* show. That seems an odd thing to make a movie from. You all remember that *Ghost Busters* show, right? With those guys from *F Troop*, and the gorilla... That was an odd premise. I always wondered what a gorilla would make of a ghost. I mean a real gorilla, you know? Like, would it even have a concept of ghosts? Of death, even?

Silence.

COMEDIAN: You don't remember that show? I guess it wasn't on very long...

HECKLER: Next!

The Chorus laughs.

COMEDIAN: Heh. Well, OK. I still have some time left, sir. Just bear with me for a few more minutes... Now, where was I... Oh, speaking of Hell, I was looking at a street map the other day. Did you know up in North York there's a street called "Lucifer Drive?" Seriously! Isn't that strange? I mean, who would want to live on a street called "Lucifer Drive?"

Silence.

COMEDIAN: A more important question, I guess, is why would anyone name a street that in the first place?

Silence.

COMEDIAN: I have a few theories. Maybe now's not the time to get into it, though...

HECKLER: Say something funny!

COMEDIAN: I don't do requests.

The Chorus laughs while the Comedian retrieves a piece of paper from his coat pocket.

COMEDIAN: I wrote down a few more things I found the other day... I thought this was interesting. This is from a publication called *Mania*, from the classifieds: "GWM, 36, 5'10", 190lbs - looking for submissive willing to engage my interest in the chemical disabling processes of various aquatic predators. I own a large, floodable studio space and an assortment of custom-made wet suits. We will submerge ourselves in a pitch-black underwater environment where I will hunt, capture, and inject you with a mild neurotoxin; after which, whatever happens, happens..."

Scattered laughter from the Chorus.

COMEDIAN: Typical gays. Always doing drugs.

The Chorus laughs.

COMEDIAN: Am I right? What is it with all these gays now? They're fuckin' everywhere, aren't they? Fucking over here, fucking over there, fucking in aquariums...

The Chorus laughs and applauds.

COMEDIAN: This is a serious social issue! I'm not prejudiced, but I'll wager this can be directly attributed to the decline in Orange Lodge membership. We're losing out values, people!

Silence.

COMEDIAN: Such a shame to see what this country's become... It's enough to make you rape your own children - or, at least, eat their clothes.

Gasps of shock from the Chorus.

HECKLER: Get off the stage!

COMEDIAN: Hold on, just wait. I still have some time left, sir. Bear with me. I'm just working some new material out...

HECKLER: Your material sucks, ya fuckin' dickhole!

COMEDIAN: Sorry, what? I didn't quite get that. Why don't you speak into the microphone...

The Comedian makes a gun shape with his fingers and points it out at the Heckler.

HECKLER: Careful where you point that thing!

The Chorus laughs.

COMEDIAN: Right, right... No, I'll be careful. Now let's see; what else, what else... Oh, speaking of pitch-black environments, any of you ever run around your apartment in the dark, not knowing if you're dreaming or awake, staring into mirrors and madly laughing from some inexplicable terror?

Silence.

COMEDIAN: Ever make a votive sacrifice to a non-existent god?

Silence.

COMEDIAN: You guys ever notice how holding a newborn kitten in your hands fills your heart with joy?

HECKLER: What the fuck are you talking about?

COMEDIAN: I'm solving crimes, damn it! Don't you fucking get that?

Silence.

COMEDIAN: You want "jokes," I suppose. Is that it? You all want to hear some jokes...? Alright, here's a riddle: How is it that the carmine wisp of a dogwood branch, glimpsed ever so briefly from the corner of your eye, can evoke the form of a whole unknown constellation?

Silence.

COMEDIAN: Give up?

Silence.

COMEDIAN: Exactly. Explanations are for cowards.

HECKLER: Hey! Andy Kaufman's dead, buddy!

COMEDIAN: Who?

HECKLER: Kaufman! He died two weeks ago. Didn't you hear? Let him take his act, or whatever the fuck this is, with him.

COMEDIAN: This isn't an act, sir. This is real. This is the land of the living! I'm alive. You're alive. Aren't we alive? Andy Kaufman's dead. Stephen Leacock's dead. Chrysippus is dead...

HECKLER: Who?

COMEDIAN: Didn't you hear? Chrysippus is dead. He died two thousand years ago. Died laughing;

watching a drunk mule eat a fig, or something...

Scattered laughter from the Chorus.

COMEDIAN: These are dangerous times, people. This is 1984! The peak of human civilization! What did Chesterton warn us of? What is it he said?

The Comedian refers back to his paper.

COMEDIAN: G.K. Chesterton, 80 years back, wrote that in the future: "It will be asked, 'Can you see the humour of an iron railing? Can you see the humour of the stars? Can you see the humour of the sunsets?' How often I've laughed myself to sleep over a violet sunset." This is 1984, people! If not now, when? We could all kill ourselves at any minute, laughing at the sky!

Confused/hesitant laughter from the Chorus.

COMEDIAN: Yes... It's a funny thing, laughter, isn't it? You know, my father used to tell me that laughing was like a cough or a sneeze - the body's way of trying to expel something. But instead of some phlegm in your throat, or some dust up your nose, a laugh happened when something really true got into your brain. Something so true that your system just couldn't stand it... I suppose crying's a bit like that, too. After all, what's that they always say? "In the end, all you can really do is laugh or cry?" Isn't that what they say? I guess sometimes the truth just isn't worth believing. I'm not really sure what's so true about a sunset, or a donkey eating a fig. I guess you had to be there... Personally, I've always felt that life's too short for truth. I'm just here to be entertained...

Silence.

COMEDIAN: And to entertain! Are we having fun tonight?

Scattered applause from the Chorus.

COMEDIAN: What a crowd! What a crowd... I should get to know you all a little better. You sir, you seem to have a lot to say. What is it you do for a living?

HECKLER: I mind my own business.

The Chorus laughs.

COMEDIAN: Self-employed, eh? No really, what do you do?

HECKLER: I try not to "do."

COMEDIAN: I see. A gentleman of leisure?

HECKLER: Something like that.

COMEDIAN: "There is a madness in me which goes beyond martyrdom - the madness of an utterly idle man!" That was Chesterton, too.

HECKLER: Never heard of the guy.

COMEDIAN: Well, he's just another corpse now. Nobody important... Any hobbies then, sir? What fills your time?

HECKLER: Nothing.

COMEDIAN: Nothing? The Devil finds work for idle hands... Nothing at all? Or just nothing you'd care to mention?

HECKLER: Nothing I'd care to tell you.

COMEDIAN: Fair enough... Could you tell me where you're from, then?

HECKLER: Nope.

Scattered laughter from the Chorus.

COMEDIAN: My, my! So many secrets! Alright, let me have a guess... Would you happen to be from Markham, by any chance?

HECKLER: Markham? Do I look like a farmer?

COMEDIAN: No... I guess I was being somewhat figurative, though. I'm just reminded of some other gentlemen of leisure, from once upon a time. Back in the Rebellion days... Do the names Badgerow, Stoutenborough, or Turney mean anything to you?

HECKLER: Should they?

COMEDIAN: What about the Hunters? Reformers? Remote Control?

Silence.

COMEDIAN: Do you remember ever hearing of the

Markham Gang?

Silence.

COMEDIAN: No? Well let me inform you, then. They were a bunch of wealthy land-owners, up north of the city. Men with a lot of free time on their hands... Men who, after getting bored with politics and fighting the Crown, turned to a life of crime - extortion, thievery, counterfeiting, murder... They were said to be the biggest organized crime syndicate on the continent, back in those days. Then they just sort of disappeared. Now what do you make of that?

HECKLER: What is this, history class?

COMEDIAN: It *could* be history, I suppose. But then again... Haven't you ever wondered why the Mob never made it past Hamilton? Why the Rizzutos and Cotronis are still up there in Montreal? With all the fuckin' guineas in this city... Who's keeping them out?

Muttering from the Chorus.

COMEDIAN: Who keeps the tax dollars out of your wallet? Who pulls the strings of your *Liberal* mayor Eggleton? Your Liberal *monarch* up on Parliament Hill? Who keeps these men wrapped in the dark folds of power?

Silence.

COMEDIAN: Have you heard about this new "civilian intelligence service" they're talking about?

What's left after crime and absolute control? What's the meaning of the moon on their republican flag? Who was Trudeau meeting with on the spring equinox? Why are there streets here called "Warlock Crescent" and "Lucifer Drive?"

Silence.

COMEDIAN: Yes, I know. I know... The trouble with believing conspiracies is you start seeing them everywhere, right? And everything becomes a part of them... But, of course, the trouble with not believing is becoming a dupe...

Silence.

COMEDIAN: Hey, like I said though, I'm not really concerned with what's true and what's not. What's "good" or what's "bad." The difference between right and wrong, to me, is of no more concern than that between a basilisk and a cockatrice...

HOST (*from off stage*): That's five.

COMEDIAN: I too have been labelled as a villain, by some. By those *powers-that-be*, and their institutions... Those men who collect "debts" for a society I owe nothing to... That I ask nothing from... Ask nothing because I can simply take! Take, because there are forces stronger than magnetism; because there are tunnels that lead nowhere else; victims born to be nothing else! Look at you people...

HOST (*from off stage*): That's five!

COMEDIAN: Any *real* criminal in this society who could truly articulate his motives would surely be found innocent by reason of insanity... Insane by reason of clarity! Freedom lies beyond this language of excuses and compromise! The "guilty" are only those who lack the vocabulary - who submit to the cowardly words of this cowardly consensus...

The Host takes the stage.

HOST (*to the Comedian*): Sorry pal, that's your time. We gotta keep things moving here.

COMEDIAN (*to the Host*): That was never five minutes! I still have some time...

The Host puts an arm around the Comedian while he reaches with the other for the microphone.

HOST: Let's here it for Alex, or whatever his name...

The Comedian withdraws the microphone and pushes the Host away.

COMEDIAN: Don't think you're going to silence me! I know who runs the nightclubs here! I know who runs everything! I'm not afraid...

HOST (*to the Comedian*): You've gotta give me that mic back, pal.

COMEDIAN (*to the Host*): Oh, really? You almost sound like you're gonna do something about it.

HOST (*to the Comedian*): I will if you don't give me that...

The Host advances towards the Comedian, but before he can reach him the Comedian pulls a pistol from his waistband. The Chorus gasps.

COMEDIAN (*to the Host*): If I don't give you *what*? Give you *what*? You'll do *what*?

The Host freezes, stuttering some unintelligible conciliation.

COMEDIAN (*to the Host*): What's that? What are you saying? I didn't quite get that. Why don't you come and speak into the microphone...

The Comedian points the gun towards the Host's mouth.

COMEDIAN (*to the Host*): Come on! Speak! Speak into this! You wanna live by the sword, you're gonna die by the sword - and I'm the fucking sword! You got that?!

HOST (*to the Comedian*): Y-Yes! Yes! Whatever you say...

COMEDIAN (*to the Host*): What's my name?!

HOST (*to the Comedian*): T-The Sword! You're the Sword!

COMEDIAN: That's not my name!

The Comedian pulls his trigger and the Host slumps dead to the floor. Then, after an appropriate period of silence...

HECKLER: The *fucking* Sword!

The Chorus laughs and applauds.

End.

Taken with permission from: *Sock - Six Plays by J. Ross Clara*; Publican Press (Toronto, 2003).

CITATIONS

The existence of a world previous to ours,
destroyed by some sort of catastrophe...
~ Georges Cuvier, 1796
'Memoir on the Species of Elephants'

Be as a planetary plague, when Jove
Will o'er some high-vic'd city hang his poison
In the sick air; let not thy sword skip one.
~ William Shakespeare, c. 1605
'Timon of Athens'

To break my neck and thy neck,
to fall into the river – that is good!
~ Anonymous, c. 1000 BC
'The Dialogue of Pessimism'

CITATIONS

QUESTION #19
Mark X.

Ontario Disability Support Program
Self Report Form - 2858 (2009/05)

This form will be used to help us understand how you feel your disability affects your daily life. Please include any information that you think will be helpful in reviewing your application to the Ontario Disability Support Program.

This information will help the ministry to get a more complete picture of your situation.

— — —

19. Please tell us how your disability affects your ability to take care of your personal needs, to participate in the community, or to work. If you need more space, use page 8:

Constant physical pain.
Mental and emotional anguish.
Low self-esteem/confidence - feeling of infantilizaion at losing control of such a basic human function.
Unable to focus or think about anything else during the day. Need to be within proximity of bathroom at all times.
Even when I am successful in relieving myself, I am sometimes at the toilet upwards of 20-30 minutes beforehand, attempting to focus and calm, lower my heart-rate, emptying my mind of all distractions.
Physical/mental toll from this act of willpower and concentration itself - from which I get only an hour

or two of relief before the process starts again.
Probable side effects - organ damage associated with
a constantly full/distended bladder which cannot be
relieved. Also the prolonged retention of urine, I
have read, can lead to a number of other severe
illnesses including urinary tract infections and
kidney disease.
Stress related to this knowledge.
Other stress-related side effects, most notably
insomnia - also likely related to first condition as
sleep is near impossible with a distressed bladder.
This places particular pressure on successful
evacuation before sleep is attempted, which then
only increases the difficulty in evacuating, leading to
an obvious vicious cycle in which neither is
accomplished.
The side effects associated with sustained insomnia,
as you will know, can be even more serious, i.e.
weakening of the immune system, reduced mental
and motor skill functions, depression, and finally
insanity as the possible results.
Suffice it to say that one in this continual condition
is not able to function properly in society, let alone
be qualified as eminently employable.

I have been talking to another psychiatric clinician at
CAMH who has agreed to submit a second opinion
on my behalf after further consultations.

— — —

As I have not yet sent this form in, I thought I
should make an amendment to the answer for #19
which I wrote the other day. I have been getting the
run-around from the psychiatrist at CAMH and my
GP - each referring me back to the other, with

neither able to agree as to whether my problem is mental or physical.

I can tell you, as I already did in my initial application, that the genesis of my condition is primarily mental. As to whether this has since manifested as a physical condition (re: the abovementioned side effects) I am not qualified to say.

In either case, the up-shot seems to be they want to put me on some sort of medication.

Although this should be indication enough that my condition is one to take seriously, I am not satisfied with this conclusion.

I suspect these doctors (and most doctors in general) of being far too eager in prescribing drugs for any sort of ailment. Additionally, the CAMH clinician has seen me for no more time than the first psychiatrist I saw (about 25 minutes over 2 visits). This hardly seems enough time to make any kind of accurate diagnosis, let alone prescribe some medication which may have who-knows-what type of further consequences.

Furthermore, just as the cause of my problems are no doubt mental, I have found the cure - when I am able to find it - to also be mainly mental.

As previously noted, in times when I am able to fully clear and calm my mind, distract my thoughts from everything, I will both sleep and urinate (not yet at the same time, thankfully - though I worry about this too).

So much of the problem, I find, is the worrying about worrying - thinking about not being able to sleep, while trying to sleep. Thinking about not being able to go, while trying to go. Then, also, in times when I am so absorbed in my concern with one, I am often able to do the other.

Nevertheless, I have not been able to find these
states of distraction very much lately.
I have been resorting to more and more elaborate
ways to divert my attention just in order to urinate:
running faucets, going in the shower (typical
associations with flowing water) - reading, or
listening to music on headset - closing my eyes and
plugging my ears to avoid any audio/visual
interference - pinching and clawing at myself -
holding my breath to the point of suffocation; at
times wrapping a bath towel completely around my
head...
Lately I've begun handling various items around the
bathroom - holding bars of soap and bottles of
bleach to my nose so as to occupy my olfactory
senses, then placing myself in precarious stances
(leaning against the wall, going from the rim of the
bathtub, standing on one leg while balancing a
plunger or toilet bush in hand) so as to engage as
much of my mind and body as possible.
These measures, however, typically work only one,
or two times, before I have to find some other
gimmick with which to fool myself.

The insomnia, too, has naturally thrown my body
clock and rhythms completely out of whack.
Though, as mentioned, at first this additional
problem was somewhat welcome (helping somewhat
in overcoming the bladder issue by simply tiring my
mind and concerning me with the more pressing
problem of not being able to sleep for days at a
time), I have gradually become accustom to this
situation, as well, and it is no longer having this
effect - in fact, it is worsening things.
I'm hoping if I can simply get into some sort of

routine this may lead to a return to normalcy. But then, this hope only puts more pressure on each attempt, etc...

I still expect this to be a temporary condition, however. Let me be clear: I am not applying for a lifetime of disability payments. Only enough until I'm able to overcome these difficulties on my own - I just don't know how long that will be.
I only know that the end is not immediately imminent, and that I am not able to financially support myself much longer - which is also greatly contributing to my worries.

— — —

Something of a breakthrough to note -
In the interest of full disclosure, and to show I am being completely honest with my application, I should inform you that I think I may have made significant progress with my first issue.
Just as I was writing yesterday of all my various attempts to calm myself before urination, it occurred that I might have been taking entirely the wrong approach all along: At my wits end, I decided last evening just to give into all of the panic of my predicament and found that, in letting go this way - to near hysteria - I was able to "let go" in the other sense. In a frenzy, just as my heart seemed about to burst, I suddenly found myself in a strange state of almost sublime indifference to everything...and then it happened.

I have since utilized this method to success numerous times throughout the past 24 hours. I was just thinking that, as doctors yourselves, you may find this information useful in treating similar cases.

Still no luck on the insomnia yet, though. After exciting myself to such levels, however, perhaps this is to be expected.

— — —

A last addendum to question 19...
It should be evidence in itself that as I am writing this nearly a week since the above (after finding I had failed to mail this off as intended) that my mind is in complete disorder. No sleep. No relief.
It seems I was too confident.

The stress of not being able to resolve this matter (both my condition and this Disability process) has only worsened things.
Despite my best efforts, things are clearly not getting better. I may resort to medication if necessary.
I am still holding out hope for a self-realized solution, though. To this end I have begun investigating certain relaxation techniques - yoga and meditation, in particular.
I have found there is a certain mental state one must get into in order to accomplish these things that we normally take for granted. It's not exactly "instinctual", nor fully intentional - but there is a degree of concentration required - an odd "focusing on not focusing", as it were.
I've come to learn that a lot of my problems are largely a function of the "autonomic nervous system" along the spinal column, which, as I understand it, operates somewhere between the conscious and sub/un-conscious realms. I have also

come across certain literature relating the autonomic nervous system to our supposed alignment of "chakras" - which, I'll admit, all sounds like so much new age bullshit, but at this point I'm willing to try anything. Really, if this whole ordeal was not so frustrating I might find it somewhat interesting, from a merely scientific point of view.

Anyways, I'm hoping the "focused calm" of meditation/yoga might help to somehow strengthen my control in this regard.

I should also note that my preliminary studies in these matters have also led to an investigation of certain related philosophies - particularly Jainism. Actually, as someone who's always had an interest in religion/mythology/etc. (if only from a purely academic standpoint) I was already somewhat intrigued by it.

I've always seen Jainism listed among the "major world religions", yet I very rarely see much material on it. In fact, I can't personally recall ever running across any books purely on the subject. Of course, there's always a chapter or two in some compilation work on Indian culture, or "Eastern Faiths" (such as I'm reading now) - but hardly ever a monograph.

I've checked the Reference Library and it only lists 5 or 6 such books - in English, anyway. Yet there's dozens on Sikhism, Zoroastrianism, Baha'i, etc. And, of course, hundreds on Buddhism and Hinduism (both a little belaboured at this point, I should think). Jainism is a relatively small religion, though - and there isn't much of a diaspora outside of the subcontinent, so that might account for its lack of popularity over here.

Still, I suspect there may also be something else going on here. The householders of this religion

apparently comprise a rather affluent minority back home - known derisively as the "Jews of India" by some. Financial and mercantile professions, as it turns out, accord best with their religious laws. But it is just these laws, when you start looking into Jainism, that really sets it apart - actually puts a lot of the other religions to shame (at least in my opinion) with respect to its rigour, its devotion, and its honesty (perhaps another reason why some would not be so keen in allowing its ideas to proliferate). The two main tenets seem to be "anekantavada" and "ahimsa" - the former I take as sort of a relativist/open-minded view of any supposed "truths" (which already agrees with my own way of seeing things), and the latter being an ethic of committing absolutely no harm to any living thing. I had actually already begun a transition to vegetarianism before all of this started, but in Jainism not only is meat forbidden, but even many things that would harm plants as well, like roots and tubers, etc. And not only eating, but even accidental killing is prevented through the wearing of face masks so as not to inhale bugs when you breath, and carrying a broom around everywhere to sweep your path clear of anything you might step on.
It's really taken seriously.
I may not quite be ready for that level of commitment - though earlier today I did overcome some slight arachnophobia to shoe a spider out the window, where normally I would have just killed it. Of course, I've never been a very religious person. I would consider myself agnostic with regards to most things. But then, most religions have always struck me as somewhat disingenuous, or compromising, if not downright silly. Either not taken seriously, or simply not that serious to begin with. Most only

seem to be justifications for various pre-existing traditions and behaviours. And yet they'll still always allow room for change - permitting this while ignoring that, as the situation merits. Always up for interpretation.

I just figure if you're going to believe something, then <u>really believe it</u> - no excuses, no negotiation. You've got to go full-out, word for word, every moment of every day.

This is probably why I don't believe in much myself. This Jainism, though, I feel it may possess a certain strictness or dedication/self-discipline I've been lacking. I guess I've just come to suspect that I may need to start taking some things a little more seriously - that my problems could stem from a certain lack of commitment to something, somehow. I'm not sure what. I may just need to start focusing that much harder.

Another aspect of Jainism I've found interesting, in this regard, is its severe asceticism. One of the penances of this faith, in fact, is "unodari" - or the reduction of food to subsistence levels (sometimes less). I have certainly already tried reducing my liquid intake so as to relieve the pressure on my bladder. This does not work as well as it would seem, though, and I have found drinking and increasing the pressure tends to help more in eventually relieving myself.

As I believe the bladder connects to the sphincter, however, a reduction in solid foods may have some positive results in alleviating the overall strain to that area. The practice of "unodari" is also said to help control over sleep, so I am very keen to see what happens.

Further down the line, the strictest Jain adherents are

eventually not permitted to involve themselves in society at all. They must withdraw from the "contamination" of human interaction (jobs, family, etc.) into a mendicant life of begging, called "bhikshachari".

I have already been leading a somewhat hermetic life - even more so since the onset of my condition. I suppose it could be argued that receiving government assistance might qualify as a form of "bhikshachari". It is probably even less harmful/contaminating than begging on the street. Just a thought.

— — —

I know I said the last addendum would be my last, but I could have sworn I already mailed this off.

I'm beginning to find it necessary to write things down now, just to keep an account of my thoughts and actions. Strangely, when one hasn't slept for an extended time, it's difficult to tell exactly when you have, in fact, slept - and when you've been awake. Being up all night, after a while, becomes somewhat dreamlike - everything's so dark and ambiguous, and then you're so tired during the day, it's easy to become confused as to what is happening, or has happened, and what may have only been a dream, or a thought - or a halucination.

If I haven't been sleeping it stands to reason I haven't been dreaming, though, doesn't it?

But if one can't dream while sleeping, one may do so while awake.

If one doesn't dream at all he can suffer a complete mental break-down. I'm sure I've read this somewhere. I'm sure it's true. I can believe it.

I've always felt dreams were important/necessary - more than that even.

Not as "omens", or fodder for analysis, or any such thing. I don't keep dream journals or anything like that. But just as a part of life - even if I can't remember them I know when I've had them. I know when they're missing. At least, I used to.

They seem more important than ever now.

I mean, so much of life is lived in the head anyway, isn't it? "Perception is reality", "you think therefor you are", etc? So if there is a reality, "out there", it's hard to say how much more "real" it is than any thought or dream - than a dream that seems even more urgent and real than any waking experience ever has.

At the moment I feel sort of "in between reality", somehow...

It's just, if things going on "out there" precede what's going on "in here" - I mean, if the stimuli/influence is external - then, just as how they say when you look at the moon you really only see how it looked a few moments ago - or a star, how it looked over a century ago - because of the time it takes for the light to reach us... I mean, isn't it the same for everything?

Perhaps it takes only a sliver of a fraction of a millisecond to perceive, but nevertheless, whatever we see is still more an afterthought than an actuality, isn't it? And further still, between the time your eye takes in the light, and the fraction of an instant before it's processed in the brain, the "real" image has passed forever, and all we apprehend is some lingering presence of the past - and isn't it so for all our senses? All our experience?

Life, it would seem, is always only lived in this state

of remembrance; and in remembrance - in the mind -
everything is conflated, levelled - made equally
"real". Experience, emotion, reflection, and dreams -
all out of time, in time, becoming the same -
becoming memories. So a dream then, in time at
least, should indeed be just as real as any other
aspect of life.
But, then, why can it seem even more real than that?

I've been giving this a lot of thought lately, if you
can't already tell. I've had a lot of time to think.
What I'm thinking now is that a dream, somehow,
may actually be sort of the final delayed reaction in
the process of this experiencing/thinking/living
continuum of ours.
If one's life is only truly in, and of the mind, then the
mind can't be all that clear to think while awake,
bombarded as it constantly is by everything "out
there" - and not only by the most explicit
experiences/recollections of the day, but also by all
those little, incidental moments in this external
"reality"; those things only briefly seen in the
periphery, or only faintly heard in the background;
things only barely read while skimming a page, or
vaguely registered while lost in a reverie.
Only in sleep, where there's nothing but mind, can
the mind clearly process all of the day's
experiences/memories - without distraction. And,
perhaps, only in sleep, where there's nothing but
mind, can the mind truly understand the meaning of
these memories, as well, and assimilate them with
all the other memories you've accumulated over
time, forming greater meanings - unintelligible in
the light of day - building, perhaps, to some ultimate
meaning at the culmination of life - unintelligible in
the light of living.

In this way, the dream life may be the only true life, where in this wakefulness "ultimate reality" is impenetrable, and "ultimate life" is only really a dream.

So you see, it could be I haven't even actually been alive these past few months. In which case, I might excuse you for not taking my application too seriously, as one qualification I assume you should have to meet in order to gain Disability is that of being a living person.
Still, I hope this will not count against me.

Alright, I should probably send this in now.

— — —

OF COURSE!
NOW ANOTHER DAMN THING!!

Everything I try to do just makes everything worse! I CANNOT EVEN BREATH PROPERLY NOW! I've already used up all of the space in this stupid booklet just to describe my "existing" conditions - and now, as you can see, I'm filling up loose leaf to relate some other new shit...

So I began practising these "pranayama" breathing exercises that are supposed to strengthen your energy/thoughts during meditation. But what these exercises have done, in fact, is only somehow make me terribly aware of my own breathing at all times so that now I must consciously regulate every single breath I take!
THIS IS INSANITY!
First urinating, then sleeping, now this?

Is there any other basic function I can ruin simply by thinking about it?
Could I forget how to walk with enough concentration? Could I make myself blind if I just focus hard enough? Could I command my own heart stop beating?
I might as well try!
A person's life just becomes too ridiculous at a certain point to keep on going.
Do you know what it's like to have to mentally force yourself to breath at all times? To have to remind yourself every single second, all day long, to do something that is supposed to come more naturally than anything?
Trying to inhale and exhale at a constant, natural rate - I have these intense cramps and chest pains now from doing this - the slightest variation and it feels all wrong...

I shouldn't have to worry about this on top of everything else!
You're not supposed to know these things...

— — —

Every day I wake up and the very first thought in my head is: "remember to breath".
It's horrible.
You can't forget something you have to do every single moment of your life.
I can't see myself ever getting out of this.

I have, at least, been waking up though - sleeping, that is. A good few days now.
My irregular breathing causes me to yawn quite a lot, which seems to make me tired.

I suppose this new problem also provides enough distraction to stave off any thoughts of not sleeping. Then, when I'm asleep, I no longer have to think about my breathing. Fortunately my body still seems capable of handling both without any conscious oversight. How long will this last, though?

Still, I have been sleeping, and I have been dreaming again.
Mundane things, mostly. What I can remember, anyway - buying groceries, doing chores, things I saw on TV, etc.
The only time I ever leave my apartment now is to buy groceries - once a week.
I'm growing less fond of that, more and more. I just want to stay inside. Away from people.
Stay in bed - asleep.

— — —

I sense that I dreamt something important last night - but I can't remember what.
Anything important I seem to forget.
There are stretches where I forget my problems, lost in thoughts of other things, living normally again - but I always end up reminding myself somehow.

It feels as though I've had all the austerities of a penitent thrust upon me. I suffer for some unknown sin - struggle with some unknown demon, or god, day after day - cut off from the world in monastic solitude, never having taken a single vow.
I'd just like to think I deserve this somehow, for some reason.

Perhaps I have brought some of this on myself. I'll

admit I've been playing with things I don't truly understand - for mostly selfish ends, having none of the reverence that should underpin such things.
Of course, I'm no monk or ascetic - not a "tapasvin", as in the Sanskrit.
The most I've been prepared to do is stay in bed, between my sheets - to remain here, in sleep - to dream only of sleeping.
Still, I can't help but feel there may be something to this. I was closer to a solution, I think, while in that earlier frenzied, panicked state. But not really "panicked", though - just taken to certain extremes.
I may have to go further somehow. But in a more controlled manner.
Radical - but relaxed...?

I've actually been researching the topic, seeing what's possible - what goals might be set:
* John & Yoko's Amsterdam and Montreal "bed-ins" each lasted one week. There was also a lesser known one, in the Bahamas, that was cancelled after a day due to heat.
* A British stage hypnotist reportedly placed a volunteer into hypnotic sleep for 8 straight days.
* Sufferers of Kleine-Levin Syndrome may sleep for up to 3 weeks at a time.
* Numerous incidents of people being bedridden for years due to morbid obesity, and other various illnesses. Naturally, though, I aspire more to an act of devotion than any further illness...
* The prophet Ezekiel supposedly laid on his left side for 390 days, bearing the sins of Israel; then a further 40 days on his right side for each year of Judah's sins.
* A certain Swami Maujgiri Maharaja remained standing, even while asleep, for 17 years (1955-

1973).
* Fakir Mastram Bapu sat in one spot, by a roadside in the Indian village of Chitra, for 22 years (1960-1982).
* The Christian stylite St. Simeon allegedly remained atop a pillar in the Syrian desert for 37 years, until his death. Coincidently, Elaine Esposito, the "sleeping beauty", remained in a coma for 37 years, until her death "*after going under general anaesthetic for a routine appendectomy.*"
* In 2003, car-crash victim Terry Wallis managed to wake from a coma after 19 years.

With respect to wakefulness, Randy Gardner holds the Guinness World Record for staying awake. In 1965, he went 11 days (264 hours) without sleep for a high school science project. Unofficially, though, a contestant in an English rocking chair marathon(?) apparently stayed awake for 18 days, 17 hours in 1977. It is also claimed that a Vietnamese man, Thai Ngoc, has not slept since 1976 due to a bout of fever which he contracted 3 years earlier.

I'm not sure if I should find these possibilities more comforting or concerning - what can be achieved through will vs. what can be inflicted by happenstance.
Of course, it's the will that disturbs me most - what one can bring upon himself.
What I may yet bring upon myself.

— — —

I've become somewhat preoccupied lately with these studies of strange feats and rituals - acts of ascetic sacrifice practiced among the various peoples of the world.

It's striking how universal this inclination seems to be - all the varied forms of renunciation and severity; self-denial/self-discipline, self-mortification, self-mutilation, etc... The Judaic "parush", the Islamic "zahid", the myriad hermits and flagellants of Christendom - ritual bloodletting in the Mayan priesthood, self-castration among the worshippers of Attis in ancient Greece - and then, of course, all the yogis, rishis, and sadhus of the East. Under the entry for "fakir" in my old Britannica:

"The tortures which some of these wretches will inflict upon themselves are almost incredible. They will hold their arms over their heads until the muscles atrophy, will keep their fists clenched till the nails grow through the palms, will sleep on beds of nails, cut and stab themselves, drag, week after week, enormous chains loaded with masses of iron, or hang themselves before a fire near enough to scorch. Most of them are inexpressibly filthy and verminous. Among the filthiest are the Aghoris, who preserve the ancient cannibal ritual of the followers of Siva..."

* Mahant Amar Bharti Ji, an office clerk from New Delhi, began holding his right arm above his head in 1973 to honour the god Shiva, and hasn't lowered it since.
* In 2004, Lukan Baba Mohan Das rolled 1,300km on his naked belly through India and Pakistan to promote peace between the two nations.
* In 1837, the hatha yogi Haridas was allegedly buried alive without food or water, and limited air, for forty straight days.
* Prahlad Jani Mataji, a devotee of the Hindu goddess Amba, has claimed to have lived without

food or water since 1940. In 2003 he underwent 10 days of observation at a hospital in Ahmedabad during which time he did not eat, drink, or use the toilet.
* Strabo, around 13AD, relates the story of a certain diplomat from India who burnt himself alive in Athens as a demonstration of his faith.

The Jains are no exception to these acts, of course. Their code of doing no harm does not, apparently, apply so strictly to oneself. I've learned that adherents are supposedly required to endure 22 afflictions ("parisahas") and 12 austerities ("tapas"), covering all sorts of mental and physical discomforts in daily life - beyond which there are even harsher options such as "kesaluncana" (pulling all of your hair out by hand), and even "sallekhana" (ritual suicide by fasting).

In other unexpected places, too - further east, beyond India, records of the otherwise serene Taoists occasionally sacrificing their flesh to the burning sun - and schools of Buddhism, founded upon their non-ascetic "middle-way", which still advocate "giving up the body" through self-immolation, self-mummification, or feeding themselves alive to wild animals.

Even amongst cultures with no great philosophies or religions this inclination/impulse seems to persist. Amongst the Inuit of our own country, for example - who claim "*we do not believe, we fear*", as one famously told Rasmussen - there is another quote, from a Caribou shaman named Igjugarjuk, which perhaps should be equally known:

"*Only true wisdom lives far from mankind in the great loneliness and can be reached only through suffering. Privation and suffering alone open the*

mind to all that is hidden to others."
In becoming a shaman as a child, Igjugarjuk
apparently fasted for 30 days, alone in the Keewatin
barren lands. Then, years later, when initiating his
own sister-in-law into shamanism, he had her hung
outside from tent poles during a blizzard for five
days, after which he shot a stone into her heart with
a rifle so that she might *"attain to intimacy with the
supernatural by visions of death."*

I can't help but think that there's some kind of ritual,
or rite of passage that I've possibly been avoiding
myself - skirting around. Something that may be
forced on me (if it hasn't been already), one way or
another, should I avoid it much longer.
Perhaps nothing as severe as all that - but something
more than what I've been doing...more than I've ever
done before.
That panic in the bathroom; all my escalating
diversions - it seems to be <u>pain</u>, in one form or
another, that sets things flowing.
Staying in bed feels just a little too commonplace
now - a little too comfortable. Not an austerity, but
an escape; another stunt, or distraction.
Not distracting enough.
There's something else I'm being drawn toward...
tempted into.

— — —

You know, it's funny how you can look at something
every day for years and still not really see it.
Only today did I noticed that I have a "Bemis" brand
toilet seat.
It's written right there on the lid in big blue letters, at
the hinge by the bowl - but somehow I never saw it.

It's very strange that I hadn't noticed this earlier, especially given all the time I've been spending with it recently. It's almost like it appeared there over night.

That's Bemis, as in Henry Bemis - the character from that famous Twilight Zone who survives the end of the world and finally gets time to read all those books, only to break his glasses and spend the rest of his life alone and blind.

And, of course, there I was not so long ago - money enough at last to quit my job, take some time off from the world and all its little annoyances, finally enjoy some peace and quiet...only to break my mind.

But then there's been plenty of chance to read in my case. To scour my bookshelves, the library, the internet - to fill my mind with all sorts of horrible ways to injure and maim and torment myself.

It's interesting what has ended up sticking.

For the past few days now, on top of everything else, I've been afflicted by what I believe you'd call "invasive", or "intrusive thoughts." One thought, actually.

One uncontrollable thought, chronically recurring every five to thirty seconds (in between all my regular thoughts of suffocating, insomnia, and failed urination, of course): that of grasping my left index finger, then twisting it, clockwise, until it snaps.

Every imaginary reenactment is accompanied by an excruciatingly realistic phantom pain, along with the hysterical urge to actually carry out the deed.

I think this is my challenge - my task.

That, or I've gone completely over the edge now.

— — —

It seems I haven't the courage to go through with this test...if that's what it is.

Numerous times I've found myself clutching the finger, a mere instant from wrenching it off. But something always stops me.

I was nearly prepared to amputate it yesterday - to put an end to this. I held it over the edge of my kitchen sink, under the blade of a new sashimi knife - I must have held it there for more than an hour.

"This could all end so easily" I told myself.

But in the end I just threw the knife out - along with a pair of scissors.

I've begun binding my fingers together with electrical tape now so that I can't get at it - occasionally wearing an oven mitt as well...then binding the mitt too.

Naturally this just serves to draw more attention to the issue.

I've tried diverting my attention elsewhere - thinking of breaking other fingers, breaking an arm or a leg, castrating myself, slitting my eyes open, etc. Nothing's caught on.

Only that finger, and only that method will do it seems - like a bad tune I can't get out of my head.

Of course, if I can't break a finger, I certainly couldn't cut my genitals off, or anything even more extreme.

I <u>could</u> do this, though - that's the thing.

At least, I think I could...and maybe that's why the thought is so strong? So taunting...

I could - and yet I can't.

It's almost embarrassing. Should I endure a lifetime of this grief and torture to spare a few moments of physical pain? Of what is, at worse, an inconvenient harm? To cripple, or even lose just a single finger would be a relatively trivial injury.
You can live a perfectly normal life missing several digits...

But then, maybe that's exactly the point?
If I remove this finger, why not another? And another?
Why shouldn't the whole hand be next? The whole arm? Then a foot - maybe a kidney?
Why shouldn't I continue taking myself apart, piece by piece?
With enough wit and charm one can probably get by in this world as just a head in a box.
Perhaps, then, it's not the finger that's trivial - but everything around it. My self, my life...this life, this lifestyle - this world...?
If I was truly being tested I wouldn't take any limb or appendage for granted, would I? I'd be required to use every physical resource at my disposal.
If I was truly living - independent, self-reliant - any finger, any body part would be sacred.

Yet if one did have to be sacrificed, for whatever reason, I should also have the courage to do that. Shouldn't I?
But I don't have the courage.
Not here. Not now.

All these afflictions I've been suffering from - to my brain, my body, all my natural functions - it's almost as if I'm somehow being forced to confront my own existence - being reminded, in some way, that I'm

still alive.
Or am I, perhaps, just acting out the behaviour of some trapped or abused animal, gnawing off its own paw to free itself - or destroy itself. Isn't that what they do?

At the moment, more than anything, it seems these things may have consumed my thoughts simply because I don't have anything better to think about.

— — —

"It is all very well for people to fast who cannot eat ... to walk barefoot who cannot ride, and then think themselves good. Let them learn to master the world before they abuse it."

(John Ruskin)

I don't think I have earned the right to suffer yet - to sacrifice.
To know what real sacrifice even is.
I have not respected my situation or myself. I must learn to master all...or, at least, some of it.
Something.

Look, I know this must seem like a lot of rambling by this point. It's just that I feel I'm on the verge of something.
I promise to get this into you just as soon as I've worked a few more things out.

— — —

I don't think it was by accident that the last of the great Jain teachers, Mahavira, and all of the other "tirthankaras" before him, were said to have been born into royal families, only then to renounce their lives of power and luxury for lives of strict asceticism.

True mastery requires true sacrifice, and vice versa. Of course, some of the tirthankaras were also said to have been thousands of feet tall and to have lived for millions of years - but there was apparently one historical figure, Chandragupta Maurya, who did in fact give up his throne, leaving behind the richest empire on earth to starve himself to death in a cave. I haven't that much to give up - but I figure there are certain things I could stand to lose.

This is why I'm currently writing from Taylor Creek Park.

The final life-stage of the Jain adherent is "sanyast-ashrama", where one heads out alone into the wilderness - the "tapovan".

I may be skipping ahead a little in my ashramas, but this seems a correct alternative to what I've now come to view as an idle, distracted way of life. A proper test/challenge/rite of passage/what have you.

Of course, Taylor Creek Park isn't exactly the wildest of wildernesses - but then, it's not exactly Queen's Park either. It should do for now. It's a start. I'm only really testing the waters. I still have some affairs to put in order (I still have to send this application in, for one thing), and I've been misled too many times already to assume that this will be the great antidote to all my troubles.

I must say, though, I'm already feeling rather invigorated.

Being outdoors is something I've missed.

Perhaps I'll try this for a week or two to start.

A week at least - I should be firm about that.
I've brought a box of almond bars and some bottled
water, but after these run out I'll be completely on
my own. I have no tent, no tools - only my body and
my wits.

Well, to be fair, there are one or two wit-
enhancements in my backpack, as well. I do know
enough to know that I don't really know what I'm
doing out here. The lessons of summer camp are
mostly lost to me now. So I've brought a book on
edible plants, along with the Eastern Religions book
I've been reading...and, of course, this notebook.
I'm actually already starting to regret bringing the
plant book, though - or, at least, bringing one this
thick and heavy. It's not just about edible plants, but
plant-life in general - rather more academic than
practical; hardcover, 700+ pages. It just happened to
be what I had.
Fortunate that I had it at all, I guess. I don't even
remember where, or why I got it.
I'll at least have lots of reading material to pass the
time.

It's coming on evening now, so I'm off to seek some
form of shelter.
I'd ask you to wish me luck, but by the time you read
this that wouldn't make much sense, would it?

— — —

I wasn't prepared for how dark it gets out here.
The park isn't lighted, and after sundown you can't
really see who's who, or what's what.
The cloud cover reflects some light from the city,
providing a little visibility, but on a "clear night" it

should be pitch black.

I didn't get very much sleep - should have put more effort into finding a suitable place to settle during the day. The darkness prevents you from venturing too far from the path. It doesn't feel very safe around here.

I managed to doze off for maybe a few minutes on a bench, but traffic through the park, even at night, is too frequent to get relaxed.

I'm thinking benches are not an appropriate option anyway, though. I didn't come here to be a wino - I should be truly roughing it.

I'll have to get further out into the bush today.

I spent most of yesterday, and this morning, reading my plant book and searching for edibles. Didn't find much.

I did locate a few patches of bulrush, though, which was promising. I never knew these were edible. The young stems, without the cattails it seems, can be pulled right out from their centre where there's a little white base you can bite off and eat. The first few I tried were pretty good actually - or, at least, innocuous. Like celery, kind of, but blander. The rest I found, however, had this sort of sour, earthy taste I didn't much care for. Not sure if it was because of the spot they grew in, or the time of year, or if I got a different type of plant altogether (the book does warn not to mistake these with certain poisonous irises and daffodils). In any case, it's not much of a meal. Apparently, though, the roots/rhizomes are edible too, if cooked/prepared properly. I could try them once I figure out how to start a fire out here - though that may be going against Jain ethics.

I assume I'll have to get a fire going to boil water, at least. I barely trust the city tap water, let alone this stuff. It certainly doesn't smell right.

Other than that, the only other thing I could find which is supposedly edible is tree bark, which I couldn't even chew, let alone swallow. I think it's supposed to be cooked as well, but I can't imagine it being much worth the effort (more of a last resort item, I suspect).

I couldn't even find any dandelions, oddly enough - but not that I'm too sad about that. The one time I remember eating a dandelion, probably around kindergarten, it made me vomit. Haven't tried one since.

Of course, not knowing what most of the plants are out here makes it difficult to look them up. Most of the entries in my book don't even have pictures, so I'm sure I must be missing a lot.

Of what I could identify, a lot seems to be just out of season, or not in season yet, which brings to mind something I foolishly didn't even consider - come winter there won't really be anything in season (other than tree bark) - not to mention the elements. Even now I could get caught out in the rain and come down with pneumonia or something.

Mosquitos, too, are another thing I didn't take into account. They made my foraging by the water nearly impossible. One of the 22 parisahas, as I recall, was to happily endure the bites and stings of insects. I assume this was originally accepted before any knowledge of malaria, yellow fever, West Nile virus, etc... It was challenge enough not to swat them.

A change of season would be welcome in this regard.

Of course, I still haven't committed to anything yet. I should get started on some sort of shelter, though - for now.

— — —

The underside of the O'Connor Drive Bridge seemed like a good candidate for a preliminary base camp, but I've been forced to side against it.

It is a rather elegant span, at a distance, I'll admit - that soaring single arch, those graceful spandrels... Up close, however, it's a far more utilitarian affair. Very sparse, very cold. Overall, it's just simply too simple - too minimalist. Not at all my style.

Granted, it's not entirely without charm. Its colonnade of tall, blocky piers does evoke a certain sense of grandeur - almost like the nave of some great open-air cathedral. But, of course, such could be said for nearly any bridge.

To be serious, the main problem is that it seems to be already well occupied.

At both ends of the bridge, and by the base of numerous columns, there were sleeping bags, clothing, various foodstuffs - not to mention mounds of discarded spray paint cans beneath layers of perpetually overlapping graffiti...all evidence of much transient, if not permanent habitation.

I didn't actually see any people at the time, but I'm sure I would have if I stuck around long enough. It's like a whole little village under there.

Exactly what I'm trying to get away from.

Any bridge, of course, is simply a link back to the city above. I should avoid that temptation at all costs. To be safe, in fact, I've decided to avoid all designated pedestrian areas as much as possible down here.

Fortunately, while I was up investigating one of the bridge's abutments, I managed to spot a more secluded passage halfway up the slope of the hill, where a hydro-line corridor cuts through the bush. It's off the paved walking trails, but is still navigable. There's a little path, presumably for hydro workers (but no recent evidence workers, or other walkers that I could detect), and it was along here that I happened upon the nice little thicket of sumac trees where I currently am.

I had noticed a few smaller thickets earlier on and thought they'd make a perfect hideaway if they were only a bit bigger - their leaves form this dense, encompassing canopy which hides a relatively spacious, if tangled, "inner sanctum" of trunks and branches, keeping much of the surrounding undergrowth at bay and forming a healthy bit of cover around the sides.

This one's still a bit of a tight fit, but in a pinch I think it should keep me cozy enough.

I'm just a little worried about bugs - though, so far, I've only seen a few snails and caterpillars. It probably won't be too dry if it rains, either. But at least I'm away from prying eyes - an important comfort. It does feel very secluded, very separate. Almost like a miniature forest within a forest; a little twilight world of my own.

Just the leaves, themselves, I find quite appealing - their pinnate shape has a sort of exotic, almost tropical feel. Kind of like a bushy palm tree (lending to a more authentic tapovan experience, I suppose). This seems to be an uncommon look amongst most local species. Walnuts/butternuts are the only other native trees I can think of with a similar appearance (another handy species to find, too, if it was later in the year). Ailanthus are also similar, and probably more common than either sumac or walnut (at least in the city), but apparently they were introduced from Asia.

The catalpa, on the other hand, is almost native (from the southern States) and also has a tropical air - but in a completely different way, with its broad leaves and long crazy seedpods. I've actually seen a few down here that have apparently escaped their typical caste of front lawn ornaments. Unfortunately the seeds, I've learned, aren't edible. In consulting my plant book, though, I'm pleased to find that the little furry berries of my sumacs are - assuming this is Staghorn and not the Poison variety. I'm fairly sure these are the safe kind, though. If it was Poison sumac I should probably have broken out in a very painful rash by now.

The fruits haven't much of a taste - vaguely sweet, I guess. They're likely too small to hold much flavour one at a time. Once I'm more certain these aren't poisonous, or that I'm not allergic to them, I'll try a handful.

Interestingly, the book also notes that, in the language of Victorian bouquet arrangement, "*a sprig of sumac was meant to represent splendid misery.*"
I might be tempted to treat that as slightly ominous if I didn't quite know exactly what it meant...
A curious concept.

— — —

I just had a strange dream. Strange, though somehow familiar.
Familiar because of the setting, or because I've had it before - I'm not sure.
I was either in the house I grew up in, back home, or my aunt's house. Possibly some amalgam of the two. There was some family get-together, or something, going on. I was trying to get away, by myself.

I wandered through the house, in and out of various rooms, when I came across a hidden staircase (I want to say either in the bathroom, or in a closet) which led to a completely unknown level of the house, seemingly in-between storeys.

Not a mezzanine, exactly - it was completely enclosed. And not unknown, exactly, either - it was seemingly a place I'd been to before, or knew about somehow...but had forgotten. An entire loft, mysteriously folded into the floorboards of my childhood - unlit, windowless, low ceilings - completely furnished, lived-in, but apparently not for a long time. Abandoned - or preserved...?

It's appointments, vague as they were, all looked to be from the seventies or eighties - dark and angular, faintly luxurious...lots of blacks and burgundys. It all felt very comfortable - comforting...intimate... familiar.

I was safe while I was there. That's all I remember. Then I woke up scratching.

Apparently mosquitos aren't the only antagonists to contend with out here. It seems some ants had crawled up my pant legs during the night.

I don't think I've ever been bitten by ants before. Definitely not pleasant - the bites look to be leaving a rash, but otherwise they're no worse than my mosquito bites...so far.

Deer ticks/Lyme disease, though - that's another thing to consider, I suppose. I'll have to devise some better precautions for tonight.

All that being said, however, I suppose the main thing to take away from last night's sleep is that I was able to sleep at all - uncovered, outside in the bush, with only a backpack full of books and water bottles to rest my head on, all while insects attacked my skin.

I'm a little surprised, actually. I hoped I could do this, but I'm still very surprised! This is very promising.

I am feeling challenged, occupied - <u>alive</u>.

A of those few morbid thoughts still linger, here and there, but I'm largely unmoved by them now.

Of course, I still can't get my hopes up too high. This isn't about hope.

With regards to my initial problem, I frankly haven't had the urge since I've been out here. I'm sure this is mainly due to my food/water intake being so low. Rationing aside, however, I simply haven't been that hungry or thirsty.

I suppose I may just be a little overwhelmed, still adapting to my new surroundings.

As I adapt I'm sure this will change.

I know there's a public washroom up by Dawes Road, but I'll bet going anywhere out here would be far more pleasant. Cleanliness aside, even while I was in "working order" I was never really able to use public facilities. Just the very idea, in this day in age, that we haven't moved beyond communal evacuation...I mean, I understand the practicality of such things, but even so - urinals? Still? This is still appropriate in today's society?

One of the washrooms in my elementary school, I recall, still used a trough!

Even stalls, though, are hardly any better. You wouldn't build a bathroom like that in your house - exposed on all sides at the top and bottom, with only a thin partition of aluminum, or whatever, in between. For the public, though, in front of strangers, this is all deemed to be perfectly acceptable? That's economics, I suppose.

At any rate, I should head over to see if I can at least acquire some toilet paper. I'm not exactly sold on the leaf method yet, and a few extra rolls should also help to soften my "pillow", such that it is.
I think I can afford myself at least these few luxuries while I'm out here.

— — —

Returning to my thicket, and to the topic of bugs, I was just visited by one of the strangest looking spiders I've ever seen. I wish I'd brought along some sort of entomology book to identify it - or arachnology, I guess...not that I own either.
Grey/beige colour, about 1 or 2 inches long - but emphasis on the "long" part! It was just very long and narrow, legs in a straight line, not all splayed-out like a regular spider - and front legs much longer than the rest.
This type must be unique to the wilderness. It's nothing I've ever seen in, or around the house - thank goodness! I'd probably lose it if I saw something like that crawling along the walls of my apartment.
But that's sort of the strange thing - out here it didn't really bother me that much. Something about it being in it's element, I guess. Its not some frightful alien out here. I am.

I think I've been gradually getting past my spider phobia over the last little while, anyways. I likely wouldn't have even contemplated coming out here if I hadn't. But still, probably no other fear has troubled me so much in my life.
Actually, any bug of undue size, or possessing what I deem to be an unwieldy excess of limbs, has long

been a cause for concern. Cellar spiders, harvestmen, crane flies, house centipedes, etc. - the longer the legs in proportion to the body, the greater was always my alarm.

I do recall a time though, previous to this fear, when I would actively engage such creatures. In fact, I distinctly remember, as a very young child, scouring the outside of my house, collecting all sorts of different specimens by hand to place in various jars and containers. For a while I was quite fond of confining them like this overnight - leaving them to each other's devices to see which, if any, would survive until morning. But then, not long after this, and without any apparent cause, my phobia began. Perhaps a punishment for these rather cruel experiments?

Fair enough, I suppose.

There is, I think, something to be said against them in their own right, though - spiders, specifically. I mean, they're just so bizarre - just a thing of legs - creeping along with that sinister gait, off to some dark corner to practice whatever evil they get up to. And there is a bit of evil in what they do, don't you find? How they live...deceptively, decadently. Just lounging in their webs - no hunt, or fair chase, only traps. And then, once their trap has snared some prey, it insists on even further cruelty by paralyzing, mummifying, and leaving its victim to hang and suffer until whenever the fiend feels good and ready to eat its catch alive...

Well, I speak as though I've been one of their victims myself. I know it's not their fault.

Still though, if one is to believe the doctrine of "punarjanma", or reincarnation, I suppose I may well have been their victim at some point. As one rises through all the stages of plants and animals - the "tiryanca gatis" - one may fall prey to the spider countless thousands, if not millions of times - just as I may have been so many spiders myself, over the ages.

Of course, having said that, I'm now forced to reflect on my own recent way of life. How deceptive and decadent - how evil it might have seemed, as well. Stuck there in my own little web of security and free time - this trap I spent a lifetime weaving; content to remain static in some lattice of complacency until something just happened along...all the while eating myself alive, from the inside out.

Such abject living is just the sort of thing to send one back on the path of "samsara" - back even to arachnoid realms...both predator and prey.

And apparently there are yet worse things to devolve into, regressing back to even the inanimate - the "nigoda"- to spend aeons as a grain of sand, or a water molecule...a drop of dew on a spider's web...

Perhaps, then, it's simply what I saw of myself in the spider that has always seemed so wrong, so perturbing - yet now, out here, rather small and harmless?

Might I now be ready for a reconciliation, of sorts? I suppose having a spider, or two, around would at least help to control the ants and mosquitos, et al...

Then again, I don't quite fancy the idea of one crawling around on me while I'm trying to sleep - or any other time for that matter. And if they bite, as well...

What other sorts of things are out here that I don't know about yet?

— — —

Only sporadic moments of sleep last night. I'm finding my current situation less and less comfortable.

The eclectic nature of my plant book may finally be starting to prove its usefulness, though. I've just come across this potentially helpful passage with regards to my sleeping arrangements:

"*Evergreens are an ancient ally of the outdoorsman ... the resin of many species acts as a natural insect repellent, while the soft young boughs of certain trees, such as the spruce and balsam fir, have long been the favoured bedding for many a makeshift, or bivouac shelter.*"

The text also mentions how dense groves of evergreens can often serve as suitable shelters in and of themselves...then goes off into this rather strange discursion on the subject of groves in general:

"*Both myth and history are replete with tales of sacred woods and enchanted forests. Deep, primal associations with the sylvan landscape, at once alluring and foreboding, seem to suffuse the whole of mankind. No wonder, then, that when such places are found condensed within certain special areas they can evoke feelings of almost supernatural force and significance.*
Seneca, in his Moral Epistles, *spoke of how particular ancient groves, by dint of their loftiness, seclusion, and manner of* 'shutting out the sky in the midst of open space', *can* 'awaken the god within us all.' *Indeed, the idea of a* holy grove *was common*

throughout the ancient world. To the Romans these places were known as luci. *To the Norse they were known as* lundrs. *Among other Germanic tribes there was the* ve *or* weoh, *while in the Baltic regions there was the* alka *and the* hiisi. *Likewise, the Greeks had their* temonos, *the Celts their* nemeton, *the Slavs their* gaje, *and so on. Notable examples of holy groves from history include:*

* *the Grove of Hekademia (north of Athens); a copse of olive trees originally dedicated to Athena, later to become the site of Plato's Academy.*

* *the Grove of Dodona (northwestern Greece); a stand of ancient Epirian oaks, home to the first Hellenic oracles who reportedly practiced a form of cledonomancy by deciphering omens heard in the rustling of their leaves.*

* *the Grove of Aricia (south of Rome); most known from Virgil's* Aeneid, *and Frazer-via-Turner's* Golden Bough. *Here, it was said, grew a tree whose branches allowed passage into Hades, and where the priest-kings of Diana Nemorensis would ritually murder each other for the right of succession.*

* *the Grove of Voltumna (north of Rome); spiritual/political centre of the Etruscan city-state confederacy, and sanctuary of their primary god.*

* *the Grove of Fetters (northeastern Germany); alleged birthplace of the Suevi. Tacitus relates it as a place conjuring* 'immemorial associations of terror'; *so-named because one could enter only in chains as an act of deference to the ruling deities.*

* *the Grove of Uppsala (north of Stockholm); temple and sacrificial ground of the Norse religion. According to Adam of Bremen, nine males of every living creature would traditionally be killed and hung from the trees there so as to indulge Odin. By*

*bearing this sacred burden the trees themselves
came to be seen as divine and were worshipped in
their own right."*

Interesting. I suspect it was probably this type of
discursion which originally led me to pick this book
up - whenever I did that.
Wasn't it Odin (or maybe Thor?) who supposedly
discovered writing by hanging himself from a tree?
The runes?
I wouldn't mind finding such a magical grove out
here - ideally one of the less gruesome kind, of
course.
I'm actually reminded of one particular grove back
home, where I grew up. Perhaps not a "grove" in the
strictest sense, though - rather a large semi-circle of
weeping willows. Ten, or a dozen of them, standing
in this wide open field at the rear of a school for the
deaf near my house.
I remember going there often when school was out,
alone - just to be there, I guess. I'd lay on the ground
and look up into its great collective canopy, lost in
thought amongst the trailing withes and cascading
leaves - submerged, as if at the bottom of some
immense kelp forest. I'd stay there for hours, just
thinking or daydreaming, watching all matter of
things flutter and leap from branch to branch in the
quiet ring above. It was really a place of uncommon
beauty - at least as far as schoolyards go. I actually
imagined it being created that way to somehow
compensate for those students' disability - inspiring
their other senses, I guess. I would even imagine
what it would be like if I had gone to school there -
if every day I played on that field and ate my lunch
under those trees, oblivious to all the sounds around
me. At times I almost wished I was deaf.

It was a far cry from the school that I attended,
anyway - cramped and overcrowded, out on the
other side of town. No real playground to speak of
either, as it had been taken over by portable
classrooms.

Interesting to contrast those <u>weeping</u> willows with
the Ashoka (literally "<u>sorrowless</u>") tree which
Mahavira was said to have begun his renunciation
under.

I've located it in my plant book - "Saraca asoca". It
actually looks from the picture very much like my
sumacs - similar leaves, similar form, even red
bunches of flowers in place of the red tufts of
berries.

I still think I'd trade-in my sorrowless sumacs for
some willows, though. Just a regular pine grove
would be welcome, as well. It sounds a rather cool
and inviting place at the moment - more so than
here, anyway. It's starting to get rather hot. Very
humid, all day and night.

I could do with a change of scenery, too. Anything
of interest, really. The canopy of this cramped little
thicket doesn't quite seem to inspire the same sort of
reverie as those willows did. The fact is I can
already sense an insidious kind of boredom in
staying out here. After reading for a while, then
pointlessly transcribing what you've just read, there
isn't a lot to do except wander around - keep
moving.

I'll have to wander off for a bit today if I'm to find
any evergreen boughs. This particular spot is rather
lacking in conifers. I may have to venture some
ways to find an entire grove.

— — —

Still in my thicket. No groves. Just a few trees here
and there - and I take it they weren't the kind I was
looking for. I'm not exactly sure what kind they
were, except to say that their boughs certainly
weren't soft.
Maybe I didn't use enough (or used too many?).
Either way it was like sleeping on a pin cushion, or a
bed of nails - not that I slept much, if at all.
I don't remember dreaming, anyway...though I did
remember some dreams.
As I couldn't get myself settled, I left to walk around
a bit. For the first night out here the sky was
absolutely clear, and for the first time - not just here,
but for years (since I don't know when) - I could see
a sky full of stars. More than perhaps I've ever seen
in this city. It was actually a little startling.
I guess I haven't really been away from the lighted
world, "up there", since moving here. I hadn't seen a
sky like that since I was a kid - or been startled like
that, either.
Even in its dim urban form, I've always found the
night sky to be an awesome spectacle. Just the sheer
magnitude of it - the incalculable scope and scale of
it all. Of course, that's what everyone says. But to
me its awesomeness is almost...I don't know...
Disturbingly awesome - "awful", perhaps.
As a boy I would often dream of the stars and
planets - of brighter, more numerous stars than there
already were; of bigger, more menacing planets...
Uranus the size of the moon, Jupiter as prominent as
the sun. Strange, gigantic new worlds looming over
the horizon, enveloping the sky; their satellites
entering the atmosphere like stupendous spherical
mountains - to who knows what end.
Not exactly "nightmares", per se...but I'm not quite

sure what else to call them.

Nevertheless, I've still always felt a strong attraction to the stars. I could never wonder at our ancestor's obsession with them - nor could I ever help but feel the weight of that obsession on us today - on me, at least. In just what way, I couldn't really tell you...but I do feel it.

Mahavira supposedly set out as a tapasvin "*when the moon was in conjunction with the asterism of Uttara Phalguni*"...whatever that means.

On just a purely visceral level, I suppose, I see the colossal decoration of this "starry dome" as, perhaps, the greatest work of art there is. But also the greatest anarchy, too. In a way, it might be the greatest horror to any discerning, delineating mind - that black, maddening firmament; that vast cosmic ocean, endlessly deep in every direction, both Heaven and Pandemonium in one...the mystical Zodiac, that speckled flesh of Tiamat...all that is chaos, infinite and eternal...

And yet, it's somehow the bringing to order of this chaos which perhaps has always disturbed me most. The constellations, in their way, almost bring into sharper focus the immensity and insanity of it all - monsters and giants brought to life in all their gigantic monstrosity...Orion and Hercules striding across the sky, limbs reaching for lightyears, only to be dwarfed by the likes of Draco, Pegasus, or Ursa Major...then bigger still - Cetus, Eridanus, Ophiuchus, and Hydra, spanning nearly the whole of their hemisphere, sunk below the equator in that weird underworld of obscure southern formations. You try to take them in - the neck cranes, the eyes roll, and the mind boggles until this debilitating sense of inverted vertigo overcomes you...or, overcomes me, at least.

You can perhaps tell that I was once very into astronomy - when I was young, back at home...when I could still see all this stuff, on a clear night from my backyard.
How this interest then turned itself into something of a minor phobia I couldn't really say.
Just another one of many I've had to deal with.
I'll leave you to speculate on just what subconscious role this might have played in my eventual move to the big city, with all its smog and light pollution - perhaps even on my recent quest for a grove that might "shut out the sky"...

— — —

I guess sleep finally caught up with me during the day. I'm not sure how long I was out for. Actually, I'm not exactly sure how long I've been <u>out here</u> for, now, either. This has sort of thrown me off.
It looks to be almost evening again. Is this still my third day, or fourth?
I probably should have been dating these entries.
Any sleep is good sleep, though. I can't complain.
More strange dreams again, too...
I first remember something about walking down the middle of a road, down a highway median, I think - cars whizzing by on either side, going somewhere...?
The road turns into a stream or river, the cars a forest (possibly here?) - then I seemed to end up in a different dream entirely.
Suddenly I'm standing in the atrium of some gallery or museum, looking up - very high. Ten, maybe twenty stories it seemed. At the very top, mounted on the wall, the skeleton of a great, massive whale.

A blue whale, I would guess, but bigger - too big. Too high, and too big...and then I was up there with it; up in the rafters, looking down on this thing, overwhelmed by it - by the size and the height and everything.

Then I started to fall.

Next I found myself in the basement. Somewhere deep underground, anyway. And here I'm faced with the real thing - the leviathan itself - as big as life and all at once. It's immersed in some titanic steel aquarium, swimming back and forth through this glowing brownish-green murk of brine and, presumably, its own filth.

I stand by the glass, in the shadows, in this rusting dank metallic nowhere, staring side-on at the beast - one goliath eye staring right back. Its grotesque, gargantuan baleen smile extends from one side. Its leathery, barnacled, unfathomable length stretches off on the other...and then, inevitably, I'm sinking down in there with it. Down to some unknowable fate, sensing only the unearthly presence of something dark and gigantic before I awake.

Clearly the dreams of my youth have returned - albeit now in rather metaphorical form...or rather, perhaps, the metaphors of my dreams (and of the constellations themselves) are becoming somewhat more literal...?

I've obviously been seeing things I haven't seen in years - invoked the names of things I hadn't thought about since adolescence. Things buried in the past. I've been doing quite a lot of this since coming out here, haven't I? I don't know why this is. Something about these surroundings?

I certainly haven't experienced nature like this, in the raw, since I was a child.

But then, I've never experienced nature quite this raw at all - here in the bush, in my thicket, in the wild; being always by this flowing creek, exposed under this sea of stars - insinuations of all things aquatic and abyssal.

It should probably come as no surprise that, at one time, I also indulged a fear of water (not to mention just about anything that might dwell within in).

You couldn't get me more than a few yards in from the beach when I was young - or even today, for that matter. I never really learned to swim.

The woods, on the other hand, were always more of a playground to me. A great leafy forum for tag, or hide-and-seek; imaginary adventures, expeditions... campaigns - playing at war.

Actually, that's probably what I remember most. My favourite game when I was a kid was always playing soldier, with the woods as my battleground - a gauntlet of cover and obstacles; knoll-side bunkers and fallen log blockhouses; a great tree trunk arena for the countless assaults and manoeuvres of pretend skirmishes I would fight with my friends, or even by myself.

But these memories seem mostly to be of winter - of digging into snow banks and stumbling through drifts...hard playing. Fingers numb, face crackling, throat scraping on the jagged air...carotid arteries throbbing until my ears felt like they were going to bleed.

War in general, or in abstract, always seems to conjure images of winter - snow and frozen forests - Napoleon in Russia, Hannibal in the Alps, Barbarossa... I'm not sure why.

The verdant woods, I suppose, were always a little more romantic - feminine, even - the scene of

nursery rhymes and fairytales.
Of course, that bubble's been burst a little since
being out here. It now seems more and more like a
battleground, too - a different type of war to wage.
Another solitary fight...

"*I took up my abode in the awesome depths of the
forest, depths so awesome that it was reputed that
none but the passionless could venture in without his
hair standing on end. When the cold season brought
chill wintry nights, then it was that, in the dark half
of the months when snow was falling, I dwelt by
night in the open air and in the damp thicket by day.
But when there came the last broiling month of
summer before the rains, I made my dwelling under
the baking sun by day and in the stifling thicket by
night. Then there flashed on me these verses, never
till then uttered by any:*

*Now scorched now froze, in forest dread, alone,
naked and fireless, set upon his quest,
the hermit battles purity to win.*"
(Majjhima Nikaya Sutra)

A Buddhist sutra - but uncannily apt, no?
It has been speculated that Buddha and Mahavira
were, in fact, one and the same person - having lived
around the same time, in around the same part of the
world, and their stories being so similar. But
whereas Buddha, and his disciples, eventually gave
up the ascetic battle, the Jains soldiered on.
The name itself is derived from "victory".

— — —

After another restless night under the stars I felt the
need to get moving. Pull up stakes, try my luck

elsewhere.

I thought I might give the bridge idea another chance. If there wasn't any vacancy at O'Connor I'd head further west, past Don Mills and The DVP (both entirely unsuitable as shelters themselves) to Donlands Ave and the Leaside Bridge.

I wouldn't let aesthetics influence my decision this time. I couldn't. Whereas the O'Connor Bridge is minimal in its configuration, the Leaside Bridge is strictly perfunctory - and on a massive, almost cyclopean scale. The piers must be, I don't know, 150-200ft tall. Megalithic concrete slabs hoisting six full lanes.

The only nod to extravagance is an empty truss-way running beneath the centre of the deck, which I think I remember reading somewhere was meant for a rail, or streetcar line, that never got built (though it may be just for maintenance).

What I did not remember, though, is that the bridge not only spans the river and valley, but also the parkway. The south abutment, closest to me, lays high up a hill, across the DVP, while the other sits past an impenetrable swath of bush on the other side of the Don.

The piers themselves provide no cover, and neither did anything else in the vicinity that I could see - at least, nothing I could easily get at.

I pressed on a bit further, to a large rail bridge near Pottery Road, and found even less cover there. I did, however, notice an intriguing little island supporting one of its piers in the middle of the river. If only I could have got to it without drowning in the process...

Shelter aside, around the same area I came across some other megaliths, of sorts: hundreds of metal

highway barriers stuck into the ground by the side of the DVP - almost like the city's own miniature version of Carnac, or Easter Island - yet much more haphazard...very strange!
I can't figure how they could have got that way by accident, nor why anyone would have put them there on purpose. The Druids never crossed the Atlantic, as far as I know.
This stretch of parkland is exceptionally lush and overgrown, though. One almost expects to uncover some ancient ruin or artifact along the way - some rotting temple, or toppled pyramid.
I suppose this whole city may well become as such, in time - overgrown, lost and abandoned; engulfed by the wilderness like so much mold on a stale loaf of bread...

I've considered continuing down the Don, but from where I am I can already hear the noise of subways crossing the Bloor Viaduct - and past that lays only civilization...and eventually the lake.
I should probably just head back now. It`s getting late.

— — —

I'll have a new home, at least for tonight. I've wedged myself under the centre "Elevated Wetlands Sculpture", or what you might also know as one of "The Teeth" - those odd, uprooted molar formations by the forks of the Don.
Not an ideal location, but I was running out of daylight. These shouldn't have much trouble in accommodating me, though. They are, after all, multi-purpose structures. According to their plaque they already serve double duty as both public works

of art and some sort of water purification system -
although affixed directly to one of the sculptures is a
sign warning: "Do not drink the water. NOT for
human consumption."
Nothing warning against human habitation, though.
The litter around here actually suggests that I'm
probably not the first person to take advantage of
them.
Hopefully I'm the only one at the moment.

Actually, all along the trail today I saw more
evidence of other people living out here - backpacks
and sleeping bags, pup tents and lean-tos, even what
looked like a tree fort. Never anyone around,
though. No inhabitants, anyways.
Strollers, joggers, bikers, and dog-walkers on the
other hand - they're everywhere.
Hardly a moment's peace out here. So much for
"jungle solitude".
So many seem to be in the annoying habit of trying
to engage you, as well. Always a "hello," or "good
afternoon" as they pass - as if they assume we
should share some bond merely by occupying the
same space.
Of course, they wouldn't dare try this in the city,
would they? No one greets strangers on the street
like that. But there's apparently something special to
them about us being out here together.
"We're the park people," they must think. "We're
healthy, outdoorsy... We still take time out of our
busy lives to appreciate nature - for an hour or two,
anyway. Greetings comrade!"
I have nothing in common with these people,
though...not even this "commons".
My park isn't their park. Not any more. This is no
idyllic pleasure ground for me. Not some arcadian

exercise course on which to entertain the absurd hopes of out-running death.

This is my home - at least for now, anyways. They can't possibly know this place like I do - and they certainly don't know me.

They don't know the good and the bad - the heat and the cold; the dirt and moisture; the thorns and bugs and nettles - cuts, bites, and stings; the trash...and the smells. Always that smell! Everywhere this rank, foetid stench of everything living and dying - or just decaying.

Well, I suppose a little of that might be coming me. I haven't bathed for days now.

Nevertheless, this is what I know - what I now must embrace.

But them?

You know, every so often I'll catch one of these people on break from their activities.

There they'll be, at some designated rest point - leaning on a railing, or maybe up a rock - face to the sun, arms akimbo, looking so "at one" with everything.

But then, after a minute or two, they'll turn away from the paved walking trail, the benches and waste bins and signposts, and they'll stare off into the creek, or the woods itself. Invariably, now, there comes across their face a look rather hard to describe - at once bemused and expressionless, almost stunned. They seem, for a moment, like they're remembering something - something lost or buried...

"NOT for human consumption."

There's never any real "return to nature", is there? We left for a reason.

And we've gone too far now to ever get back. Gone to the stars and empty space - comets and asteroids and collapsing suns. We must move on if only to defend ourselves. To return to nature is to embrace extinction...eventually.

Only some of us have had to return - to take the test all over again.

It could be though, I suppose, that we're all still sort of lost out here. That we've just found a little clearing in the wilderness of everything, huddled together and called it "home".

And if that's the case - if I'm still going to be lost, no matter what - well, why not just get lost as possible, right? The only way out, if there is one, must be to keep going...farther and farther...

Clearly, though, I haven't gone far enough. I haven't lived here long enough.

I obviously still have a ways to go before I can truly call any of this a "home" - my home. Before I myself appear lived-in (or "lived-on"...?)...at least to these people. That is to say: <u>unapproachable</u> - homeless.

"Henceforth Mahavira was houseless, circumspect in his walking, circumspect in his speech, circumspect in the carrying of his drinking vessel, circumspect in evacuating excrements and uncleanliness of the body, circumspect in his thoughts ... his heart was pure like water in autumn."
(Kalpa Sutra)

I am trying.

— — —

I was back in the loft again - safe and alone.
I suppose I shouldn't really call it a "loft",
though...not in the traditional sense. It isn't open
concept, as I've now discovered. This time I found
other rooms, and other levels as well.
Never really any full rooms or levels, though.
Everything seemed more like a nook or alcove,
closet or crawl space - I actually remember having
to do a lot of crawling. I mentioned how low the
ceilings are, didn't I?
I sort of get the impression of it being almost a
grown-up's play house. Somehow small, but also
big...
And always dark. I don't remember there being any
light fixtures. Still, I could see everything perfectly
well. Not that there was a whole lot to see - every
room, or nook, seemed to be a bedroom of sorts...or,
at least, had a bed.
So they might, I suppose, as they all felt just as snug
and relaxing as the next. But I didn't stop to relax in
any one spot. I just kept exploring, restlessly, always
finding yet another room, then another and another...
Then, at last, a staircase like the one which led me
here to begin with. Up and out of the loft, into one
last bedroom - my bedroom, in the house I grew up
in.
It was just as I remember it: my bed, my desk, my
dresser (though possibly rearranged in some now
obscure way). And my window where I could look
out over the backyard - just as I remember it - over
the fence into our back neighbour's house; into the
room of the girl who used to live there.
But not everything was as I remember it. Off to the
sides, where more fences and more suburban houses
should have been, were instead laneways like the
kind you'd find here - and different houses, also of

an inner-city style. Then further in the distance, past my neighbour's house, the city skyline. Not the current skyline, though - at least, not as it is today - but perhaps how it might appear 100 or 1,000 years in the future - colossal, interminable; sprawling off past the horizon in every direction - rising up higher than the clouds.

From my room I could survey the whole of this metropolis - megalopolis - mega-conurbation, in fact! For it seemed not only to integrate my own hometown, but also everywhere in between, and beyond: Hamilton and Kitchener swallowed up along the way, then queerly combined with every other city I'd ever been to - Vancouver and Ottawa shoe-horned somewhere into the distance; Clearwater Florida, where my family used to vacation, merging with the harbourfront; the towers of Atlanta, Cincinnati, and Detroit looming across the water along a drastically condensed/relocated Interstate 75.

The little backyard slice of my old neighbourhood seemed to be the only residential area left. Everything else was high-rises, expressways, factories, and shopping centres, piled one atop the other in this vast, impossible urban complication...

You can imagine the jarring shock of waking up back in the wild after such a vision.

Not quite as jarring, though, as waking up someplace other than where you went to sleep! Somehow I found myself back at the Leaside Bridge, resting against one of those piers - and I have absolutely no recollection of moving, or being moved there.

Just to be sure I did, in fact, move I had to recheck my notes - and to do that I had to recover my

221

belongings, back at The Teeth where I assumed they would be.

I have no prior history of sleepwalking. None that I know of, anyway. I have no idea how else this could have happened though.

I'm not aware of any of the causes of sleepwalking. Could low-nutrition be one?

I've only recently regained a bit of my appetite since making-do on just one or two of these almond bars each day. Funny that this should occur right as I find myself down to the last one.

I'm still not very confident about subsisting on whatever nature might provide out here.

I suppose this is where the test really begins.

— — —

I've been searching further afield than ever, now, for wild edibles. Completely off any paths or trails - trudging aimlessly through knotted snarls of bush; wading waist-deep through dense morasses of ferns, weeds, and God knows what else.

I've gone so completely off track that I'm now a bit disoriented.

Of course, I know I'm still somewhere in the middle of the city. As untamed as it all might be, if one goes far enough afield out here you're eventually bound to hit another trail, or bridge...or even someone's backyard - so I'm not too worried.

All along the top of this ravine, in fact, I can see the rear-ends of people's homes. I've also noticed many feel little need to bother with a backyard fence. They must assume the wildness of their ravine to be security enough. It wouldn't be much trouble from where I am, though, to just walk right into one of their living rooms...or kitchens.

Actually, while consulting my plant book earlier, I learned that "ravine" itself is originally from an Old French/Middle English word for "plunder" or "robbery" - from the Latin "rapina"; related to such other words as "rapine", "raving", "ravenous", and "rape".

There are other precautions besides fences, however. Dogs seem a popular, and presumably effective measure. I should say they don't seem to take very kindly to me.

I can hardly pass any canine-held property without sending its resident sentry into wild fits of barking. Nor, actually, had many passed me, along the trails with their owners, without frantically barking should they happened to spot me, just minding my business alone in the woods.

There seems to be something alarming to them about a man in the bush. Some ancient watch-dog instincts, no doubt - always on guard for trespassers. I suppose my strange, woodland behaviour must give off some fairly suspicious vibes. Quite admirable, in a way...if also a little annoying.

Beyond even that, though, I'm beginning to wonder if, perhaps, they sense in this behaviour a little of what I'm beginning to sense in myself - a certain growing detachment from civilization, from humanity - those very things which must have drawn them out to us from their primeval wolfpacks, all those generations ago.

Of course, I'm not quite ready to forsake all the products of society, just yet. I have my clothes, my books (hopefully another pathway, or set of directions, too). But more and more I can see myself leaving much of the rest behind - leaving their makers, and the crucible from which they proceed. If at times, after all, I happen to benefit by the rays of the sun, must I then seek to reside in its nuclear core?

I must be close enough as it is, already!

It's so very hot...

But these conditions should only fuel my resolution. I've become increasingly determined to manage out here - alone, away from people.

Their presence is already beginning to fade into the background - their forms concealed by trees and distance; their sounds echoing through the buzzing din of wildlife, like the faint bleats and whinnies of any other incognizant animal. Their noise often seems now to have no more semblance of language than that of their dogs.

But could it be I'm simply no longer making the effort to understand? Might I even be gradually losing this ability (hopefully my writing is still making sense)?

If this is, indeed, what "man's best friend" has been picking up on, it may be a rather distressing thing to sense in one of their companions.

Again, quite admirable...if also a little concerning.

Not long after I set off down this ravine, in fact, I noticed two rather large (and unaccompanied) dogs monitoring my progress with some concern. They were across the stream - well back at first, but keeping pace and steadily closing distance.

They both seemed to be of the same breed - though one was grey while the other was brown. I'm not sure what type of dog they were. I could only describe them as "hound-ish". They were domestic looking: well groomed, not at all feral - probably belonging to some household nearby, though I couldn't detect any collars (and certainly no leashes).

Oddly, unlike the other dogs I've encountered, these ones didn't bark or growl - they simply pursued in silence. Still, I doubt this was out of friendship. As they drew closer I caught in their eyes a strange, disquieting look of almost confused indignation - perhaps even surprise; of ones who had just stumbled across some unexpected intruder...or unfamiliar quarry.

On and on they tracked me like this, for what seemed like a few hundred yards - stopping when I stopped, resuming when I did the same. Their relentlessness was, in a word, unsettling. I can't say I ever felt in any real danger of actually being attacked by them, but I did get the distinct feeling of being, well, stalked - if not hunted - and that it was perhaps only this confusion I saw, possibly of their own domesticated, civilized nature - that detachment from the primeval wolfpack - which spared me.

Then again, they may have simply been ushering me off whatever they perceived their territory to be. It was certainly a large territory, though, if that was the case (I should likely not have become as lost as I currently am if it wasn't for their pursual).

I may have also inadvertently spared myself by stumbling into inhospitable grounds. They finally called off their chase after I passed into this patch of...something. "Tangle-bean" I call it, for lack of a proper name. Some thick jumble of vines up to my knees, with these pointy little pods everywhere, trapping and tripping-up my every step. More than once I nearly had the boots pulled right off my feet! I could barely make any headway through it myself, so I can imagine it being near impossible for even a large dog to tackle.

If these are in any way edible I should have a

veritable feast at hand. The landscape is absolutely covered with it. But the problem, as always, is identification.

Nothing else in the immediate vicinity looks very promising. It's too late in the season for fiddleheads, and all the mature ferns are apparently carcinogenic. I don't know what most of this other stuff is. A book on mushrooms would have been helpful it seems. There are numerous large growths of various description out here - each a potential snack or death sentence as far as I know. Not really sure on the Jain edicts regarding fungi, either...

I may just have to start trying things.

Not all is bad news, however. I did manage to find some excellent shelter. Fortuitous, really, as I'm far more tired than hungry at the moment.

Just past the tangle-beans, I began noticing some scattered bits of rubble, here and there. Then, in the middle of a clearing, I discovered the remnants of what I'm guessing must have been some sort of out-building - maybe even a little house.

What did I say about finding ruins out here? Not exactly a temple or pyramid, but what it lacks in mystique it more than makes up for in utility. Just a couple of crumbling walls - what appears to be some mixture of stone and concrete - but with enough overhang in places to keep the weather off.

Not that I wouldn't welcome a little weather at this point. It's so damned hot...so humid. A downpour must be long overdue.

— — —

I caught myself this time - I just woke in mid-stride, heading right up the side of the ravine; backpack on and everything, ready to go wherever I was going...wherever I am now...even more lost than before - deeper into the ravine (which seems to have become deeper itself). I'm a good way up from the stream now, yet the rooftops around me have all but receded past the crest above.

How I managed to get this far somnambully without killing myself is anyone's guess.

It's almost more logical to assume that I'm actually still asleep. This would have to be an exceptionally lucid dream, though...even if I really don't feel quite awake, either. Not in the normal sense. I feel a little strange. These surroundings feel strange.

It must still be the middle of the night, but it's uncommonly bright - either that, or I'm beginning to see in the dark.

If the moon is out I can't tell. It looks as though I might have finally found my pine grove - a good stand among these other trees, anyway. Some elbow room, at least.

I would try going back to sleep, but who knows where I'd wake up next?

— — —

I've gradually come-to with the sun. It would seem this wasn't a dream after all.

I'm here, indeed, amongst a great many pines...and a forest floor I can actually see. There's cliffs and crags and open space - rather more alpine than jungle, now. Room to stretch out, or to move - and view where I'm going...look out over where I've been.

I'm still not sure how far I've come. I can't make out any sign of the ruin I went to sleep in. I can only reckon it's downstream, somewhere. All these evergreens fall back into another quagmire of deciduous bush downstream. They look to continue a fair ways upstream, though.

If I follow the current I'm sure I'd eventually end up somewhere around where I started - at the Taylor, or the Don again. I've never really been one for retracing my steps, though. Especially when they lead back through all that mess.

I think I should stick to the open ground, while I still have some.

Of course, there is still this matter of finding something to eat.

These pines may be accommodating, but they're useless for food...though, I may drawing an unhelpful distinction between what's "edible" and what's "palatable". The needles are apparently an excellent source of vitamin C - if you can choke enough of them down.

I'd just like to find some proper sustenance, that's all. I should consider this entire venture a failure if I can't manage to pull together at least one descent meal out here.

In fact, I'm not leaving until I do.

I still think I should be OK, for a while. I find just writing like this helps to keep my mind off my stomach...that is, when I'm not writing about food, anyways. It at least keeps me from more foolhardy activities. More than once I've actually had the notion of heading up to the top of this slope and pilfering someone's vegetable garden...

The third great vow, though, prevents any form of stealing.

But then, of course, the first is not to kill:
"*I renounce all killing of living beings, whether*

*subtle or gross, whether animate or inanimate. Nor
shall I myself kill living beings, nor cause others to
do so, nor consent to it in any way. As long as I live,
I confess and blame, repent and exempt myself of
these sins..."* (Acaranga Sutra)

Yet I have killed.
I confess and blame myself - it's simply impossible
not to trod on snails out here.
There are absolutely millions of them, everywhere. I
always try to watch my step, but when you're
traipsing through undergrowth, being chased by
dogs, moving at night...it's just impossible. Ever
since abandoning the pavement, I've heard the crack
of a shell under one of my boots at least a dozen
times. I couldn't hazard a guess at how many (or
what else) I've trampled in my unconscious
wanderings.

That is the point, though, isn't it...? Hopefully... I've
not <u>consciously</u> killed any of these beings. It should
only be the intent which is the actual sin, shouldn't
it?
I can't seem to find any clarification on this in my
book.
You would think, though, even with brooms and
masks and all other precautions, accidents are still
bound to happen...lapses in vigilance bound to
occur. And then there's things which are simply
beyond any control. One can be the most serene
endurer of bites and stings while awake, but in sleep
the body will instinctively swat a pestering fly, won't
it? Or simply roll over on something.
And even if one was to somehow keep himself
constantly awake and alert, staying perfectly
motionless so as not to disturb even the smallest dust

mite, his very own immune system would still be slaughtering bacteria and viruses by the trillions. We are killing, every one of us, every moment of the day - just by living. And if one realizes this, is this very realization itself not a conscious consent to murder? If a truly circumspect Jain was truly serious about not killing anything, wouldn't his only recourse be to kill himself? And not by some long, drawn-out starvation - but immediately! This is the paradox...

— — —

I've managed to find some further writings on the matter in a commentary on Buddhist monastic laws (as it's somewhat of a "cousin" philosophy, I suppose it may be applicable) - "*With regard to animals it is worse to kill large ones than small, because more effort is required. Even where effort is equal, the difference in substance must be considered. With regard to killing humans it is worse to kill more virtuous ones than less.*" (Buddhaghosa)

In terms of both effort and virtue, I suppose the ritual suicide of a monk must be the worse case of all. Strange, then, that so many should do this. Buddhism seems filled with these kinds of contradictions. All very "zen", I suppose... To begin with, Buddha claimed he never even wanted to start a religion - to be worshipped as a saint or a god (everything he spoke against in the Brahmanism of his time) - yet he nevertheless deigned to ascend his soapbox and teach a group of "disciples" his "special wisdom". Clearly this "enlightened one" had a very poor understanding of human nature if he could not see how this would only result in another cult of ceremony and dogma; fables and legends; clergies, hierarchies, and various divergent schools - each with their customs and costumes, relics, idols, shrines, temples, and all the other forms of silly distraction which constitute the Buddhism of today.

Of course, I'm sure it was conveniently added in later that he did, in fact, foresee that all this would come...but I guess, hey, "whatever".

He still maintained that the path to enlightenment was aidless and leaderless - that nirvana can only be self-realized - and that all people have this ability within them, no matter their station in life. But then, what of other lives? Those ones which it is supposedly less harmful to kill. Could other animals achieve this enlightenment, too? Apparently not! Apparently they lack both the "physical and mental qualities" required to perform this trick - to meditate and be "at one in the moment". Yet any beast is clearly more "in the moment", living here and now, than any bodhisattva ever was. What monk has ever been more "unattached" than a bear in the woods - more still and focused than a wildcat fixed on its prey? Which zen master's mind was ever more empty of thought than that of a woodlouse, or river oyster...a worm...or a snail?

Further still, Buddha did not deny the existence of gods. Indeed, he was tempted by demons during his spiritual quest, and claimed men could be reborn as "devas" just as they may be reborn as bugs. Yet, what is a man but a bug to a god? What mental, physical, and other untold qualities might they have over us?

What arrogance, and ignorance - what elitist caste fetishism to assume that only now, in this anointed human form, might we attain to ultimate reality...that whatever he claimed to see or feel under the rose-apple tree is all that's worth experiencing.

I think maybe, somewhere along the way, both the Buddhists and the Jains got things a little wrong. Certainly, both have since become mired in the irrelevant raiments of traditional "religion" - worst of all, acquiesced to the degenerations of a laity. I mean, why even countenance an easy way - a deferred liberation in some other life? What's wrong with right here, right now?

They speak of "ahisma", though surely less harm is done each day on the floor of a slaughterhouse than in a bank, or stock exchange. The irony that such wealth should proceed from sect of homeless beggars... But then, what room is there for irony in the realm of "anekantavada"?

I may need to look farther back for guidance - to a common ancestor - their "shramanic" roots of less organized asceticism. To the Kapalikas, Carvakas, and Ajivikas of times past, who it would seem chose rather to become extinct than corrupt themselves through all these varied modern fragilities.

The problem, of course, is there isn't much left to learn from them - and what does remain mostly comes from the writings of their dubious rivals. There is one passage in my book, however, from a certain Purana Kassapa - apparently a contemporary of both Buddha and Mahavira:

"*To him who acts, O king, or causes another to act, to him who mutilates or causes another to mutilate, to him who punishes or causes another to punish, to him who causes grief or torment, to him who trembles or causes others to tremble, to him who kills a living creature, who takes what is not given, who breaks into houses, who commits dacoity, or thievery, or highway robbery, or adultery, or who speaks lies, to him thus acting there is no guilt. If with a discus, with an edge sharp as a razor, he should make all the living creatures on the earth one heap, one mass of flesh, there would be no guilt thence resulting, no increase of guilt would ensue. Were he to go along the south bank of the Ganges striking and slaying, mutilating and having men mutilated, oppressing and having men oppressed, there would be no guilt thence resulting, no increase of guilt would ensue."* (Samanna-Phala Sutta)

Allegedly Kassapa later drowned himself in a river... He seemed to accord mostly with the Ajivika school, from my understanding of it. Supposedly they had more of a fatalistic/determinist view, where no karma would ever accumulate beyond what you are born with - regardless of your actions, good or bad. As for karma itself, it is apparently only that which binds "jiva" (sentience, life, spirit, etc.) with "ajiva" (the lifeless, material aspect of this world) - perhaps not unlike that which science seeks to bind energy with mass (if I understand either concept correctly). But it is only through asceticism that one might shed his predestined karmic allotment.

I suppose this is what I still don't quite understand in any of these shramanic philosophies, though - their end-game. Their "moksha", or "mukti", or "samsara". This oneness/emptiness, liberation/transcendence of karma/ajiva, of rebirth and ego - of "the self", of life...of everything.
How exactly would this state differ from any standard, scientific definition of death - plain old death? Or, at most, if any experience remains, from

what might be more commonly imagined/feared to be death - some dark perpetual existence of paralyzed, semi-conscious nothingness...an incessant dreamless sleep from which one never wakes? They all assure you, of course, that this will be no condition of endless torment, but rather one of "eternal bliss". Inexplicable, incommunicable "bliss", mind you...but "bliss" nonetheless.

So many in the realm of science, too, seem to propagate a notion of "bliss" - only here, in this world, with the universe being some great amusement park of non-stop wonder and discovery. Any truly scientific, unbiased examination of their "discoveries", though, only ever seems to reveal a world that simply just "is" - where "wonder" is merely a euphemism for ignorance, and learning is its own reward because, frankly, nothing else ever could be.

Still, the scientist seeks to conquer this ignorance, even though his very happiness depends on it - offering only some pale vision of eternal dumbfoundedness, and endless hollow surprises.

The shramana, on the other hand, offers total knowledge of this hollowness, all at once - renouncing any form of happiness or pleasure, here, to seek some other ultimate, unknowable "bliss", off in the beyond...

It would seem Buddhism is not alone in its contradictions. Perhaps its "middle-way" is simply the lesser of all these hypocricies?

But still, there is this:

"I have been an ascetic of ascetics; loathly have I been, foremost in loathliness; scrupulous have I been, foremost in scrupulosity; solitary have I been, foremost in solitude ... Of all the spasms of pain that

*have been undergone through the ages past, or will
be undergone through the ages to come, or are
being undergone now by recluses and brahmins,
mine are pre-eminent; nor is there aught worse
beyond. Yet, with all these austerities I fail to
transcend human limits and rise to the heights of
noblest understanding...*" (Majjhima Nikaya Sutra)

Ah Buddha, you boastful charlatan. You may have
learned nothing after 6 years of suffering, but then
what of 7 years? What of 70? What might you have
learned from a lifetime of pain? You will never
know that.
I've been at this only 6 days, and you have nothing
to tell me. Only I will know whatever I come to
know. Your ignorance is yours, and mine is my own.

From what I can tell, the wisest man in all these
scriptures was the first person Buddha ever tried to
teach - an Ajivika named Upaka.
Buddha bragged to him of how he achieved nirvana,
to which Upaka simply replied: "That may be so,"
and walked away.
Ha ha...fuck you Siddhartha.
However fruitless this may otherwise be, asceticism
at least serves to punish our pretentious humanity.
This heat and this hunger will keep me humble...if
nothing else.

— — —

I walked for a ways along a ridge through the pines,
presumably still towards the source of this stream
(wherever that might be). Then I came to a juncture
where I could either head up or down - up the
precarious rim of a cliff face, or back down into the

bush, along what appeared to be a faint animal trail. In my weakened state, I opted for the downward path - back into the jungle.

My footing just isn't quite a sharp as it was. None of my faculties are, I'm sure. More than once in this terrain I've nearly snapped an ankle - besides which, my toes and heels have now become a mass of seething blisters. I simply can't trust my step with anything too treacherous at the moment.
Furthermore, as much as I would have liked to test the comfort of laying out under those evergreens, if I'm still going to be wandering around while I sleep it's probably best that I do so away from any steep ledges.
That said, the low road was not without its surprises, either. Once again my ramblings led me to the site of a ruin - though nothing quite as extravagant as the previous ones. Just a simple stone pillar this time, halfway down the trail - around 3 or 4 feet high. Maybe part of an erstwhile wall, or gate...I'm not sure. Perhaps just a pillar, lone in itself.
Small as it was, in the thick of all this wilderness it did tend to stand out like a monument. It may have been the Bahubali at Sravana, or Kanishka's great stupa out here...or perhaps something more anonymous and ageless, as if born from the earth itself. A strange, pseudo-natural obelisk, there only to induce marvel...or, at least, to rest against while I tempted sleep once more...to move, to be transported once more - from the base of that little column at the bottom of a ravine, to a view from the top of the sky - high in the tallest tower of that city I'd seen from my bedroom...now looking down from an improbable observation deck...seeing things in reverse, from within, from above...seemingly at the

very edge of the atmosphere...floating on the brink
between this teeming grey expanse of urbanity, the
airy-blue curvature of the earth, and that endless
black concavity of space...

From this soaring vantage it seemed I could now
take everything in...I could not help but take it -
everything, against my will - clinging desperately to
the floor of this dizzying precipice; the summits of a
million other jutting towers swirling below me;
every star and planet in the galaxy circling low
overhead.

As I tried to gather myself, recapture my bearings, I
fixed my gaze in the distance, scanning the limits of
the city - and as I did, I somehow managed to send
myself away to certain locations - one after the other
- one atop the other - both there, at ground level, but
still hovering in the sky. There I'd be on the streets
of some far-off suburb...and there I'd be, on my
teetering perch above the world, remotely surveying
the whole of this outlandish creation.

I feel I could almost begin to draw a map of the
place. I'm just not certain I could ever finish...

To the east I recall a great arcing road, flanked on
one side by stores and homes, and on the other by a
vast open park, stretching off without any
discernable end. To the west were broad, tree-lined
avenues, ornamented with various strange statues,
fountains, and other such things - all of vaguely
classical affect...which gradually gave way to a
rather more derelict district, sunk into a deeply cut
valley approaching the waterfront. Northwards I saw
grand flights of industrial office parks, steadily
fading into a network of cozy little suburban streets,
seemingly locked in a sort of perpetual evening. All
of it new, yet familiar, as always...

And then, to the south, at the very fringe of the sprawl, that which was most familiar: my neighbourhood, my house, my room - me, looking back at myself.

Once again, much of it was just as I remember (however reliable my memory is at this point) - all the "courts" and "gates" and other cul-de-sacs just as they were; the school for the deaf at the top of my own crescent; the shopping plaza right in the centre of things; and then boundless fields and farmland in the undeveloped township beyond.

But still, there were also those things that just shouldn't quite be - those laneways again, with strange other houses hidden within them...and then, in my neighbour's yard across the street, a little stream sprouting forth and heading back into the city.

There was - or is - a little creek in a park nearby...as well as the river that flows and forks downtown. But they're not of the same system, and not of this configuration.

This was another waterway. The one I'm at now, perhaps?

I descended somehow, down through this tower...and also, it would seem, through time as well. Floor by floor, each level revealing some architectural element of my past - the halls and lobby of my apartment; the various rooms of previous homes; then all the offices I had worked at; and then my university, and my highschool...or some vaguely similar institution of learning, still hundreds of feet up there in the sky.

As if to confirm my location, I began searching for my old locker - but I couldn't remember which floor it was on. So I kept spiralling down and down, through this interminable series of hallways and stairwells, always past the same empty classrooms it seemed...down and down past countless blank chalkboards and vacant desks, through the forest of highrises still looming outside...then down, at last, to the forest floor...and down further still, beneath the tower, and the city itself...only to come out into another, subterranean city.

Or, perhaps, something more akin to the PATH complex - only instead of being some dim, convoluted ghost-mall, this seemed to have the feel of a great bustling market, overflowing with shops and stalls peddling every manner of ware...and within them even further, hidden emporiums, tucked away, one behind the other in a sort of infinite commercial regress...in which somewhere, within this byzantine chain of nested stores, I was diverted from my aim - whatever that now was - drawn to the dusty leather bindings of an antiquarian bookseller; lost underground, amongst a prodigious maze of shelves, in the pages of some now ambiguous tome...and finally, back out here, amongst the bugs and bramble of yet another obscure stretch of ravine.

I suppose I can't even be sure if this is the same ravine...the same creek or stream, or any of it now.

I suppose I can only keep heading towards the source.

— — —

Earlier today I finished my last bottle of water. Instead of just throwing them out, I probably should have been refilling them at those drinking fountains back in the park.

I must have figured dehydration was a worthier
penance than lugging all that fluid around.
Easy to figure when your bottles are full.
Master yogis aside, I think I read that you're
supposed to be able to go a couple of weeks, or so,
without food - but only a couple of days without
water.
In this heat I couldn't risk one, so I've fought my
way down to the stream to gamble with whatever
microbes might be lurking therein.
Luckily enough (at least, I hope this is lucky), I
ended up by a little cascade where the water tumbles
over a few feet of rocks. I know that fast and
flowing is better than slow or standing with regards
to what you should drink, so I took a chance and
filled my empty bottle.
The water is cold and clear, and doesn't seem to have
any strange odour/taste.
So far I'm not feeling any ill effects.

The stream widens out at the top of the cascade
where the sides have been reinforced by a stone
embankment. I take this as a sign that I may be
nearing civilization again, though the walls of the
ravine are so deep here that I can no longer see
what's above them (...odd, as I would think the
ravine should get shallower, and the stream
narrower, the further up it I go).
Nevertheless, I'm fairly content to be here at the
moment. The water itself is quite shallow, and cool,
and I've made my way out to a large outcrop of
rocks in the middle of it - just far enough from the
banks, it would seem, that the mosquitos and other
pests won't bother me.
The only bugs out here, at the moment, are
dragonflies. Three types, it appears: lovely small

ones - iridescent blue with black wings; another, slightly larger kind - chalky-white in colour with striped wings; and then those big, almost prehistoric green ones - "darning needles", I think they're called. I remember seeing some as a child that I could have sworn were a couple feet long...

But then, everything seems bigger to you back then, doesn't it?

— — —

Comfortable rocks. I got so relaxed out here I must have dozed off for a bit...or passed out.

I woke up in the same place, though, so I gather it wasn't a proper sleep.

It's still day. It's still hot. I'm still tired.

I really should find something to eat - <u>soon</u>.

I thought I had located some rhubarb near the bank, just a moment ago. I was taken in by the large leaves - very large - more than twice the size of my head, in fact!

On closer inspection, however, it turned out to be burdock. Odd that two completely different species should be so similarly conspicuous.

My plant book notes that burdock actually goes by the alias of "wild rhubarb" in certain places - though it's completely inedible (at least if not thoroughly cooked first). This name refers only to the "lesser burdock", though. By the size of its leaves I'm guessing my find was of the "greater" variety.

It must have the largest leaves of any plant out here. I can't think of any close competitors...

Hogweed, I guess, might compare (also, incidentally, known as "wild rhubarb" to some - though the leaves are of a completely different shape...and the whole plant is toxic, even to the touch).

Not surprisingly, none of these species are actually native to this land - and, I must say, they do seem to have a somewhat foreign appearance to them...those leaves.

I can't imagine this reserved and modest soil producing anything so inordinate, or superfluous - so out of proportion...so obscene.

There really is, the more I look at them, something mildly offensive about their size. Something...I don't know quite what...

They seem, I suppose, to be almost flaunting themselves...mocking the landscape...possessing almost an undue abundance of life...overabundance ...as if somehow imbued with the ludicrous threat of sudden animation...

Of course, they are hardly the most blatant offenders in this regard. Not according to my book. To find these you must sink to even warmer climes - to suffer the compound foliage of the cycads and monocotyledons, as well a certain giant ferns; to the fan-like protrusions of the "talipot", or "coco-de-mer", which attain spans of over 15 feet!; or the fronds of the "sago" and "sugar palm" which may reach upwards of 30!

None of these, though, even begin to approach the monstrous "raffia", whose leaves have been measured up to 80 feet in length - more than twice as long as the tree itself is tall!

Mind you, I would sooner stand to encounter any such feathery, segmented limbs than I would some of the smaller, yet infinitely more disturbing specimens of undivided blades - creatures such as the "Colocasia gigantea", or the "Alocasia robusta", which may impose 20 feet or more of pure, unadulterated, hideous leaf...thick and dripping with gluttonous vitality...lurking there, on the unspeakable verge of something dark and tyrannical...

But surely I have more important business than ruminating on such absurd things.
I should get moving again. This spot has become somewhat distracting.

— — —

I've been making record headway along the ledge of this embankment - the closest thing to a real path I've had since getting lost. The only problem is I still have no idea where all this headway is leading to.
East York, North York, Scarborough... Oshawa... Niagara Falls?
As I turn each bend I hope to find some indication of my whereabouts, yet every new vista just reveals more of the same...perhaps only a little darker, and a little deeper.
Scaling the walls of this ravine now would require a serious feat of mountaineering, yet there is little along its heights to suggest it would even be worth the effort.
There is, nonetheless, still plenty of evidence (or, at least, reminders) of people...somewhere. Rubble and garbage strewn about everywhere - bricks, and tiles, and concrete blocks; coils of rebar and planks of wood; discarded bikes and shopping carts; TV sets and fax machines; all manner of paper goods and beverage containers...clothes, and toys, and even what looked to be the better part of a car!
One of the more common relics I seem to find are

expired credit cards and driver's licenses - various
other forms of ID. I could well emerge from here as
an entirely different person, if I was so inclined...

Of natural artifacts, the most prevalent seems to be
skulls - and all of the same creature, it would appear.
I'm guessing they're raccoons...possibly skunks. Sort
of what I'd assume a cat's skull would look like -
about the same size, two large fangs in the front...
I suppose they could be cat skulls, too, for that
matter. I did see a stray prowling around out here, a
day or so back. Fortunately I've not yet encountered
a skunk. I haven't seen a carcass of either.
If I do find a corpse it's usually a raccoon's. I've
found quite a few, actually. One particularly grizzly
example was torn right in half - the upper portion
completely gone, devoured by something.
It's a bit unsettling to imagine there are things out
here that can do that. I recall a few signs warning of
coyotes, back in the park. Haven't encountered any
of them...yet.
I wonder if there could be wolves here, too? Maybe
just those dogs I saw before?
Most of the raccoons I find, though, are more or less
whole. Dead of natural causes, I presume - eaten by
worms instead of wolves...and still not quite as
common a sight down here as they are by the roads,
"up there".
Predators aside, they seem to stand a better chance
of dying from old age in the woods. You'd think such
an urban animal would have better learned to avoid
man's contraptions by now. I'd see them all the time
around my neighbourhood. I'd see them get hit, too -
by accident, and on purpose.
Not very popular with the locals, but I never minded
them myself.

How could you, really? Halfway between a dog and a cat, with those little humanlike hands - adorable. Maybe just a bit too fearless...

Whenever I'd come across any, up early to get groceries or whatnot, they would just stop whatever they were doing and stare, until I moved on. I could get pretty close sometimes, if they were in a garbage bin or something. They'll stand their ground, up to a point.

Yet something like a squirrel, on the other hand, you can't get within 30 feet of without it darting up the nearest tree. That's a city animal who's learned to live in fear.

I'm not quite sure what they're so scared of, though. They aren't really treated as pests. Not like raccoons, anyway. And I don't think too many people ever try to eat them.

Then again, pigeon's are another city animal, and they'll walk right over your foot if they feel like it. They're certainly treated as pests, and I think they were even brought here, initially, as a food source. I'm sure I read that somewhere.

Of course, they can always just fly away.

Still, you'd think they'd be more wary, simply out of instinct.

Now that I think about it, ducks are also fairly acclimatized to humans. They're everywhere out here, and I find they'll stay pretty calm within about 10 feet, or so. Geese, too, will let you get right up to them before taking off - or hissing at you. Perhaps they're just used to people feeding them bread crumbs, etc. But you'd think they'd be more concerned with people feeding on them, as they're often apt to.

It's strange - every once in a while I'll spot a heron

out here, as well, and if it happens to spot me back, even at a good fifty yards, it'll be up and off immediately. Now when's the last time anyone ever ate a heron? Maybe back in the court of Nero or Caligula, or someone like that. I've certainly never seen one in the supermarket.

Do people hunt them for sport? Just by their size you'd think they'd have less fear than a pigeon or duck, regardless.

Then again, it may be that fear which has kept them out of the supermarkets all this time.

It's just strange how docile so many "game" animals seem to be, by comparison - almost compliant in their role as prey.

I actually saw a deer out here, not long ago - on the other side of the ravine, up near the top of the ridge. It was far off, but not too far. It noticed me and stared for a bit - striking that classic "in the headlights" pose. But then, I guess, it determined I wasn't a threat and just carried on, perhaps to forage in someone's backyard...up there.

I tell you, with a gun you wouldn't have needed to be any sort of master marksman... That deer wouldn't even expect it. It's probably never seen a hunter out here.

Even without a gun, perhaps...but that would take some doing. Some strength, and real devotion. Just to fashion a suitable weapon, or trap - then to implement it. Perhaps days of preparation and planning, then stalking, waiting...and then doing it again.

I gather this is how it must have been...how it still is for any real predator - dedicating so much time and resources to the hunt...to killing. It must consume the vast majority of one's life - become it's very purpose at some point.

But then, of course, it can also be so easy - any unsuspecting pigeon...or even all those snails.
If only I had a taste for escargot...
I suppose, at times, one merely has to make the effort.

— — —

At last, a beacon - or so I thought. One of the city's Parks & Forestry information signs, toppled over by the bank, slowly being claimed by the flora.
I hoped it would tell me where I was.
I suppose it did...

"Riparian Zones: A riparian zone is the intermediary environment between the land and a river, stream, pond, or lake. A well vegetated riparian zone is important for a number of reasons. It helps protect water quality and provides habitat for wildlife. They are natural buffers, helping filter surface water and moderating main water body temperatures. Root systems help stabilize soil and prevent erosion. Plants act as sponges, reducing and slowing the amount of water that enters a river, which is especially important during storm events."
(Metro Parkland Naturalization)

Even if the sign did give a location, I suppose it shouldn't have been trusted. There's no reason for it to be where it is - here, in the middle of wherever I am.

Of course, there's no reason for any of this garbage to be down here. But it is.
I figured it was all just dumped - but "storm events"...

There was that big storm last summer, wasn't there? And all that flooding, 3 or 4 years before. Flooding every few years, to some extent, I'm sure. And then flooding to the most extreme extents - 1878, Hurricane Hazel...

All this debris, all those ruins I've been seeing...that would make sense. The flotsam, jetsam, and wreckage of so many storms.

How much might have been ruined or relocated over the years - taken away in every deluge? How much has simply vanished? Houses and bridges, people and whatnot...washed away...in the flow of time...a whole invisible city lost in these "riparian zones", somewhere between here, and now...and then.

I guess I could have been washed away myself, at any moment - caught in a flash flood while out in the middle of this stream...or anywhere, really, in these ravines.

But then, maybe I have been...?

Perhaps I've vanished, too. Deceased. Become just a memory of myself...just another apparition in these haunted valleys. If not washed away, then faded - from starvation, heat exhaustion...devoured by wolves...?

But I'm still hungry. I'm still tired, and very hot. It seems I've yet to shed this skin. But still...

Ever since I was a child, you know, I've held a strange notion that perhaps I have died - that, in fact, one dies constantly, countless times, but just never knows it. That one might perish at every turn they might, yet simply continues on from their moment of death, seemlessly, into some other life, indistinguishable from the last, never any the wiser. Of course, this may simply be a way of trying to reconcile the fact that I've done so many foolish things - this latest venture notwithstanding - that I probably should have died on more than one occasion.

I believe, though, certain theories of modern physics, with multiple dimensions and other such things, might yet bare these suspicions out.

And if so, where does that leave all those other timelines - all those departed?

Here, in these ravines and ruins?

If I turned back, might I stand to catch the spectre of my very own ghost?

— — —

Onwards, and something new to note: the stream has forked, requiring me to head back down in the water to investigate.

It's quite shallow here, enough that I can walk right along the bed, rock to rock. The channel itself, however, is now a lot deeper - the stone walls being just taller than myself, giving the feel of a large flume, or sluiceway, rather than anything natural.

Without a thought I've headed to the right, up the narrower of the two branches. I'm not sure what guided this choice, but, lost as I already am, there probably wasn't much point in deliberating between the two.

Nevertheless, this was apparently the wrong choice. I've hit a dead end - but a spectacular one.

The water has just opened up into a rather large pool, above which stands quite a edifice - some great concrete outfall, maybe 10 feet across and at least as tall.

Truly a bulk of menacing workmanship...brutal, dark, and cold; discharging this torrent of effluence from its vast, grated maw.

It's quite a jarring sight in the midst of all this.
Almost alien... It reigns over this site with a nearly
religious intent - like an altar, or some sanctorium
for a strange and unknown god. Or, perhaps, even
more like the god itself...eyeless, earless, with only
that mouth - spewing forth its liquid dictates in a
never-ending stream...

...this stream, that I'm in now - that I've waded
through, and drank from.
Where does that mouth lead to?
A sewer?
Is that what this is?
Have I been wallowing in sewage all this time?
It still looks clean enough. It doesn't smell...but,
perhaps, I've just grown accustom to all the foul
odours out here?

Then again, this may simply be the tributary of some
long buried river. That's not so uncommon in this
city, is it?
In this city, though...
Underground... The market...what was it?
Might it have been in the sewers, too? Was it even a
market at all?
I seem to remember it now more as...a station? Yes.
But not just a station - a terminal, or junction...a
great confluence of every line in the city...level upon
level of intricate transfers...and me rushing through
them all as I tried to find a certain platform...to
where?
To a track without a subway, or train - an abandoned
line that I remember heading down, on foot...down
through these endless darkend tunnels and
passageway...perhaps even through a system

drainage pipes? Perhaps... But then out, at last, on
the tracks again - out into an open corridor...this
colossal arcade of iron and steel...a titanic, rusted
framework of some crumbling industrial age...
I must have followed this decay for hours...for
days...until I was then above ground, walking across
a massive bridge spanning the city below...the
pinnacle of some grand collision of infrastructure,
with expressways, railways, and all other means of
transit interweaving like a thousand towering roller-
coasters - pathways radiating in every direction...
Overcome, I scrambled back to grade...and then
back underground - into the grey, hollow chambers
of some crypt, or catacomb...somewhere dark, cold,
and dank.
Into the sewers...again...
Perhaps?

So where does that hole lead to?

The pool looks far too deep to negotiate. These
walls, too steep to climb and get a look inside.
If I wasn't so damned weak and tired... So...
This day feels like its gone on forever. Now I have
to head back, down the other fork...to wherever that
leads me...

— — —

Where the fuck am I going? Where is any of this
leading to?
This bottomless, endless, despicable gully - this
monotonous trough of earth...
What do these stone walls build toward? Where does
this water empty?
Who am I talking to?

I don't even know what compelled me to start keeping this preposterous journal - how, or when this pointless conceit began...

Why am I still writing now? To what end? For what audience? Myself? There's no one else here...

What am I trying to immortalize? What could be so important anymore?

All these trivialities and irrelevancies - if only I had been more trivial! More meticulous. Coherent! It would, at least, be somewhat useful if I happened to record some directions - a map - mentioned somewhere how the hell I got out here...

I've gone back and started reading from the beginning, but I can't make any sense of it - some bewildering notes on something I was going to write, then page after page of inscrutable reasons not to...or, at least, I think?

Somewhere in the middle of all this there must be some clue as to where I am!

These other books, here, what good are they? Some ponderous bestiary of all this horrid, useless vegetation - interspersed with arcane expositions on Myrkvithr and Gargaphie...on Actaeon transformed and set upon by his hounds...on Cernunnos, "dindshenchas", and Celtic bog rituals...on Pan begetting "panic" from the bowels of his dreadful groves - and on, and on...

Then this other book, going back farther still, surely beyond any useful departure point. What practical guidance is to be culled from this venerable "Rig Veda"? What am I to make of such beginnings as this:

"Then was not non-existence nor existence; there was no realm of air, no sky beyond it. What covered

in, and where? And what gave shelter? Was water there, unfathomed depth of water? Death was not then, nor was there aught immortal; no sign was there, the day's and night's divider. That One Thing, breathless, breathed by its own nature; apart from it was nothing whatsoever. Darkness there was; at first concealed in darkness this All was indiscriminated chaos."

What am I to make of any of it?
I have darkness. I have hunger. I have unbearable heat, and no way out.
I'm circling...

They say its not about the origin, or the destination, but the journey. Perhaps, then, its not the story, but the writing...and the reading...
But what's it all about when there's no end, or beginning, in sight for either?
If someone else should ever happen to find this - is reading this now, in some future unknown...I don't know. What can I say?
If none of this was for my benefit, then perhaps it will be for your's.
In any case, I have little else left...
Shall I continue?

— — —

It's so hot now I can't even move.
The sun's pressing down, sapping every bit of strength...yet still remains invisible.
In all this darkness and shade... I'm so weary.
I've just been laying here, on the rocks, in the stream...half wet, half dry...stewing.

I've been laying here, watching some bird on the rim of the channel. It's a type I've not seen down here before - but still, a bird like any other... Small and brittle, bright and composed...summing me up with its wide, expectant eyes.
Fixed in his beak is some bit of refuse, plucked from the wire mesh holding these walls together. I watched him struggle some time to wrench it free, tearing off countless little pieces before claiming the greater whole of it.
Now he just stands there, watching me back...as if judging whether I, of all things down here, will be proper witness to his victory...

And now, like that, they're both off. The bird and his prize. Escaped to the heavens, carried aloft...up to some sunlit makebelieve, far beyond this chasm.
This place I can't seem to escape...where I'm imprisoned...indentured - to this slog, this ravine...to that hateful, boiling star...
If I could just stay here, unmoved...like one of these plants - feeding from its rays, drinking in the moisture rising off this stream...growing strong.
But I can't.
The relief of water is too fleeting. Too faint.
All relief is just that.
Even if I were to shed these clothes, immerse myself in the depths of that pool...
If I knelt down on the shore of this reality and plunged my head into that dark, babbling cistern...eyes open...stagnant…catatonic…
stratified... If I was reduced and returned…slowly compressed, cell by cell...back into the senseless, the organic...back further still...to one prostrate dimension...flat and inert...wraithly dense...singular.
Pressed back into the loop - that indecipherable

string of endless inconsequence - the static, eternal, atrophied existence of this... Of whatever <u>this</u> is... However cool, however frozen...only then to be pulled back out by the heels...to endure it all again... If I were to make it as far as winter, when all these birds and plants have retreated and declined...when the exposed corpse of nature is laid to rest beneath a soothing, numbing pane of snow... It would only melt, and fade, then start again.

Only this heat, and that hidden sun - only its vagrant beams shining here on this stone, on the water...only this is real.

This concrete, and the space in that hole - these are the only natural things in this whole sunken world.

I should tear every bit of green out by its roots! Put this whole fucking gorge out of its misery! If only that would.

If only I had the strength to move...to live, or to die.

— — —

In his Epic, *Gilgamesh, together with Enkidu, are said to have cut down the great Cedar Forest, home of the gods, so that they might earn immortality.*
In 1590, the Italian nobleman and composer, Don Carlo Gesualdo, razed the entire forest around the Palazzo San Severo in Naples where he had murdered his wife, and her lover, so as not to have the trees conceal his shame.
Controlled forest burning was a common land-management technique practiced among numerous primitive cultures, including the American Indians and Australia's Aborigines.
The deforestation of Easter Island is thought to have led to the almost complete extinction of its

native population by the early 19th century.
*During WWI it is estimated that half of the
productive woodland in Great Britain was felled in
supply of the war effort. Further untold millions of
acres have been lost due to 'scorched earth' tactics
in various conflicts throughout history; from
Caesar's clearing of the great Hercynian Forest
during the Bello Gallico*, to the mass strategic*
retreats through Russia's vast wilderness in the last
World War.

— — —

I see now that I'm too weak. I have suffered too
long. All that I seek had been gifted to me...and I
forsook it.

Everything I've said and done, up til now, must be
disregarded.
They are nothing but the empty actions of any
martyr...any victim. The vain accounts of any fool
fighting strife, or injustice...the trite, impoverished
outcries of a war-torn land.
Those who struggle, those who sacrifice, are nothing
but mislead. No one with dreams of a better life can
understand. A dream is simply a distraction to keep
you asleep.
The poor and downtrodden, the "oppressed" and
"disadvantaged" - they can know nothing of
truth...of reality. They have nothing to say on this
issue.
Not them, nor the common. Not the humble, nor
middle class. Not even the mildly rich can truly
perceive. No middling, commonplace man could
ever penetrate this existence. No one engaged by the
distraction of mere survival can ever know anything

of life...this gratuitous life.
Only the most affluent, the most idle - the most
decadent, debauched, and bored can afford such
luxury. Only a life completely without distraction
can plumb the full abyss of its own being.
It cannot help but sink in it.

If I cannot be a jina, a buddha, a tirthankar, then let
me go fully back the other way - back to my palace
and my kingdom. Back to opulence and abundance.
To wealth beyond all measure.
Everything beyond measure...beyond counting. to
absolute zero.
take me there and I'll tell you something of it...

— — —

somewhere there's a house at the top of all this...
a great mansion of innumerous rooms...
i can see it, grand and stately, on the crest of a vale...
overlooking the solitude of this sullen, fulsome
dene...

all around its property rolls off far and wide, defying
the presence of any neighbours... a place where you
can stand alone, barefoot and innocent, on the cool,
dewy grass of your own convictions...
up where everything has a pure and naive sort of
beauty... where the sun shines so brightly that it all
nearly disappears - unfocused, in a crystalline haze...

the servants and caretakers will have gotten quite
comfortable by now... they've just settled right in
while the master's been away...
they must surely feel protected by that broad, empty
space... by all these sheer, unassailable walls...

they must think themselves safe from any returning,
from him coming back to reclaim what he paid for...

but what they've forgotten - what those heights and
sunlight can't reveal - is what lies underneath...
at the very foundation...
that open portal

...that passage
...that void

the hole at the bottom of everything

no stream leads to anywhere but its source, or its end
while neither lead anywhere except to themselves
as all in between dies, at last, in completion...

Taken with permission from: the files of Dr. S.A. Sandringham,
BSc, MD, FRCPC; Dentonia Health Centre (Toronto, 2009).

*Thus we see that the whole world is but a world of grief
and misery, all the people of the whole world are but
grieving and miserable people, and all the living beings of
the whole world are but murdered beings. The azure
Heaven and the round Earth are nothing but a great
slaughter-yard, a great prison.*
~ K'ang Yu-wei, c. 1900 AD
'Ta T'ung Shu'

*Jesus said "Whoever has come to know the world has
found a corpse. And whoever has found [this] corpse, of
him the world is not worthy."*
~ Didymos Judas Thomas, c. 100 AD
'The Gospel of Thomas'

*Mount thou upon the ruined mounds of ancient cities and
walk around; behold the skulls of those earlier and later
times. Who is the evildoer, who is the benefactor?*
~ Anonymous, c. 1000 BC
'The Dialogue of Pessimism'

CITATIONS

HYPOGRAPHS
Various

The optimist proclaims that we live in the best of all possible worlds; and the pessimist fears this is true.
~ James Branch Cabell

The optimist thinks that this is the best of all possible worlds, and the pessimist knows it.
~ Julius Robert Oppenheimer

Sometimes a pessimist is only an optimist with extra information.
~ Sayyid Idries el-Hāšimī

Man, at least when educated, is a pessimist.
~ John Kenneth Galbraith

Pessimism, when you get used to it, is just as agreeable as optimism.
~ Enoch Arnold Bennett

The record of history [...] indicates that man is quite as enthusiastic about living in hell as in heaven.
~ Herman Northrop Frye

For whatever the tortures of hell, I think the boredom of heaven would be even worse.
~ Isaak Yudovich Ozimov

Boredom in the midst of paradise generated our first ancestor's appetite for the abyss [...] That appetite, a veritable nostalgia for hell, would not fail to ravage the race following us and to make it the worthy heir of our misfortunes.
~ Emil Mihai Cioran

*The hell to be endured hereafter, of which theology
tells, is no worse than the hell we make for ourselves
in this world...*

~ William James

*Why must we seek hell in an afterlife? Is the hell
surrounding us, and the hell within, not sufficient?*

~ Adolf Josef Lanz

*Hell hath no limits, nor is circumscribed
In one self place; for where we are is hell,
And where hell is, there must we ever be.*

~ Christopher Marlowe

*Which way I fly is hell; myself am Hell;
And in the lowest deep a lower deep
Still threat'ning to devour me opens wide,
To which the Hell I suffer seems a Heav'n.*

~ John Milton

*A weight hangs on a hook and in hanging suffers
that it cannot descend [...] Its life is this lack of its
life. If it no longer lacked anything – but were
finished, perfect: if it possessed itself, it would have
ceased to exist.*

~ Gedaliah Ram Michelstaedter

*Good for nothing, there to be used, ready for
anything, it is alive. It lives on the fringe of
existence its own disturbing, absurd life.*

~ Jean René Bazaine

*Life, like a dome of many-coloured glass,
Stains the white radiance of Eternity...*

~ Percy Bysshe Shelley

Our very life is our disgrace.

~ David Henry Thoreau

Life is divided into the horrible and the miserable.
~ Allan Stewart Konigsberg

Life is an incurable disease.
~ Abraham Cowley

Life is one long process of getting tired.
~ Samuel Butler

Life is just one damned thing after another.
~ Elbert Green Hubbard

Heraclitus, the philosopher, out of a serious meditation of men's lives, fell a-weeping, and with continual tears bewailed their misery, madness, and folly. Democritus, on the other side, burst out a-laughing, their whole life seemed to him so ridiculous...
~ Robert Burton

The laughing man knows more of his mirth than the thinking man knows of this thoughts.
~ François-Marie Arouet

Knowledge is laughable when attributed to a human being.
~ Herman Poole Blount

Human beings possess the weapon of knowledge in order to make life bearable [...] and with knowledge they can make the very intolerableness of life a weapon, though at the same time that intolerableness is not reduced in the slightest.
~ Kimitake Hiraoka

He that increaseth knowledge increaseth sorrow.
~ Koheleth

CITATIONS

Pain is the root of knowledge.

~ Simone Weil

It is pain that sets thoughts to thinking.

~ Paul Carus

*Suffering is the sole origin of consciousness [...]
consciousness is the greatest misfortune of man.*
~ Fyodor Mikhailovich Dostoevsky

*For it is the destiny of man that he should seek to
take upon himself the burden of understanding, and
to move in the comprehension of his works and the
consciousness of his crimes.*

~ John Stewart Collis

*The source of every crime, is some defect of the
understanding; or some error in reasoning; or some
sudden force of the passions.*

~ Thomas Hobbes

*There are crimes of passion and crimes of logic. The
boundary between them is not clearly defined.*
~ Albert Camus

*Thoughtcrime is a dreadful thing [...] It's insidious.
It can get hold of you without your even knowing it.
Do you know how it got hold of me? In my sleep!*
~ Eric Arthur Blair

*I go to bed, and I wait for sleep as a man might wait
for the executioner.*

~ Henri René Albert Guy de Maupassant

*It was true that he had made his own bed, and he
understood the justice which required him to lie
upon it.*

~ Anthony Trollope

The principles of justice are chosen behind a veil of ignorance.

~ John Bordley Rawls

If we lift the veil and look underneath [...] we shall discover much emptiness, darkness, and confusion; nay, if I mistake not, direct impossibilities and contradictions.

~ George Berkeley

The result of this confusion manifests itself in the paradox that the reality in which we live is determined by unreality which we believe to be real because it is rational.

~ Otto Rosenfeld

It is to be believed because it is absurd [...] It is certain because it is impossible.

~ Quintus Septimius Florens Tertullianus

Sometimes it feels as if the essence of living is the sensing – indeed, the savoring – of paradox.

~ Douglas Richard Hofstadter

Life is therefore also a contradiction [...] and as soon as the contradiction ceases, life too comes to an end...

~ Friedrich Engels

Know then, proud man, what a paradox you are to yourself.

~ Blaise Pascal

Since we live solely from and by contradictions, since life is a tragedy and the tragedy is in the perpetual struggle without hope or victory, then it is all a contradiction.

~ Miguel de Unamuno y Jugo

There is nothing at all anywhere in which contradiction [...] cannot and must not be exhibited.
~ Georg Wilhelm Friedrich Hegel

There is nothing that does not contain contradiction; without contradiction nothing would exist.

~ Máo Zédōng

Nothingness is being, and being nothingness [...] Our limited mind cannot grasp or fathom this, for it joins infinity.
~ Azriel ben Menahem

Our knowledge can only be finite, while our ignorance must necessarily be infinite.
~ Karl Raimund Popper

We live on a placid island of ignorance amidst the black seas of infinity; and it was not meant that we should stray far.
~ Howard Phillips Lovecraft

Man's unhappiness, as I construe, comes from his greatness; it is because there is an Infinite in him, which with all his cunning he cannot quite bury under the Finite.
~ Thomas Carlyle

O God, I could be bounded in a nutshell and count myself a king of infinite space, were it not that I have bad dreams.

~ William Shakespeare

*My eyes close in order to see without understanding
the dream in the infinite space that recedes before
me, and I have a sense of the doleful march of my
hopes.*

~ Eugène Henri Paul Gauguin

*It is through dreaming that man communicates with
the dark dream by which he is surrounded.*

~ Jean Nicolas Arthur Rimbaud

*This hard wall that bars me from my freedom, these
very tablets on which I am writing, and all the
substantial realities [...] appear no better than the
offspring of a diseased imagination, or the baseless
fabric of a dream.*

~ Edwin Abbott Abbott

*We have dreamt the world. We have dreamt it as
firm, mysterious, visible, ubiquitous in space and
durable in time; but in its architecture we have
allowed tenuous and eternal crevices of unreason
which tell us it is false.*

~ Jorge Francisco Isidoro Luis Borges Acevedo

*Do ye know the terror of him who falleth asleep?–
To the very toes he is terrified, because the ground
giveth way under him, and the dream beginneth.*

~ Friedrich Wilhelm Nietzsche

*I always feel as if I'm living out a dream – a
hideous, fiendish nightmare – that I'm not a man but
a shadow, some creature that's fit for nothing.*

~ Lyova Zasetsky

*What is man? What is he not? He is the dream of a
shadow...*

~ Píndaros

"Why, you're only a sort of thing in his dream [...]
You know very well you're not real."
"I am real!" said Alice, and began to cry.
"You won't make yourself a bit realler by crying."
Tweedledee remarked...

~ Charles Lutwidge Dodgson

A dream will always triumph over reality, once it is
given the chance.

~ Stanisław Lem

It is all a dream – a grotesque and foolish dream.
Nothing exists but you. And you are but a thought –
a vagrant thought, a useless thought, a homeless
thought, wandering forlorn among the empty
eternities!

~ Samuel Langhorne Clemens

We live as we dream – alone.

~ Józef Teodor Konrad Korzeniowski

He desperately wanted to wake from this terrible
dream, to break through the hopelessness of mental
stagnation, to find the world clear and
comprehensible instead of having to grope for every
word he uttered.

~ Aleksandr Romanovich Luria

When, in some dreadful and ghastly dream, we
reach the moment of greatest horror, it awakes us;
thereby banishing all the hideous shapes that were
born of the night. And life is a dream; when the
moment of greatest horror compels us to break it off,
the same thing happens.

~ Arthur Schopenhauer

There is the great awakening, after which we shall know that this life was a great dream. All the while, the foolish think they are awake, and with nice discrimination insist on their knowledge [...] I, who say that you are dreaming, am dreaming myself.
~ Zhuāng Zhōu

Life would not be a dream, and all experience would not be an illusion, if I abstained from believing in them.
~ Jorge Agustín Nicolás Ruiz de Santayana

I have just described a sensation of anguish and dream, the anguish seeping into your dreams, and this is how I imagine agony seeps into you, and perfects itself finally in death.
~ Antoine Marie Joseph Artaud

Death seems a long way off. Is this not shallow thinking? It is worthless and is only a joke within a dream.
~ Yamamoto Tsunetomo

Every pleasant fantasy, every thought of the future in which I indulge [...] consists of death, and nothing else. And in this desire I am no longer troubled, as I used to be, by the memory of dreams.
~ Giacomo Taldegardo Francesco di Sales Saverio Pietro Leopardi

Death is no dream.
~ Samuel Levine

I waited 'til dreams, like my heart, were all broken. The flowers were all dead and the words were unspoken.
~ Herbert Desmond Carter

There'll be flowers for you, flowers and a coffin.
~ László Jávor

I do not dream. I do not think anymore. Close to the grave, all grows lighter.
~ Johann Wolfgang von Goethe

Yet still the light does not suffice. So the moth plunges entirely into the flame, while his companions await his return to recount the experience [...] How then shall he return to explain what he is now in full possession of?
~ Abū al-Muġīṭ Husayn Manṣūr al-Ḥallāǧ

And when I summarily reflect upon those sinister mysteries by which a human being disappears from the earth, as easily as a fly or dragonfly, with no hope of return, I find myself nursing keen regret at probably not being able to live long enough to explain properly to you what I do not myself pretend to know.
~ Isidore Lucien Ducasse
